# OUT THERE

# Out There

## ADRIEN
## STOUTENBURG

THE BODLEY HEAD
LONDON SYDNEY
TORONTO

*Out There* was first published in the U.S.A. and this British edition has been reproduced by photographing the American text. To have altered the American spelling would have added greatly to the expense of production and would have meant increasing the published price of the book. We have therefore retained the American text, believing that readers would rather have the book available in this form than not at all, and so such spellings as *color* (for British *colour*), *somberly* (for *sombrely*) and *skepticism* (for *scepticism*) will be found throughout the text.

*To Timothy Lee and Timothy Michael*

# OUT THERE

# CHAPTER 1

THE attic was a place of perpetual twilight in spite of sunshine or electric lights. Even at high noon, as now, it seemed that dusk had arrived, an impression heightened by the black clouds scudding across the mountains and the first plops of rain on the roof. The Heads, as the children always thought of them, looked alive in the gloom, especially the rhinoceros with its small eyes gleaming. From his window bench Patrick could watch both the rhino and the neon lights of the distant gambling casinos housed under the great thermoplastic dome that covered all of the new part of the City. On top of the astrodome a red beacon swiveled against the dark sky, its beam regularly stroking the attic to light up the rhino's square, sad mouth and the two horns on its snout. Just beyond hung the Arabian oryx, the shadows of its antlers like those of a sharp-petaled flower.

There was little sound except for hard, heavy raindrops and the *tap-and-thud* of Knobs sitting on the floor in the farthest dim corner, tossing jacks and a rubber ball over and over. She was always doing that, so the others scarcely heard. Sometimes it seemed that it was the only thing she knew how to do. The children seldom remarked on it. Knobs couldn't help it, as Aunt Zeb regularly reminded them. "You have to remember what happened to her."

Patrick shifted on his window seat, growing impatient. As the leader of the group, he had made his speech and was waiting for some response from the others. He counted on Sylvie to speak up; she was always so certain of herself and quick to challenge his ideas. He was a whole year older than she, being thirteen, but that didn't stop her. However, now, like the others, she sat brooding, tugging at a long, light-brown braid that dangled to the belt of her white shorts. She had a sulky look, which was normal.

Lester, Patrick's age, had assumed what he claimed was a yoga position directly in the center of the floor, legs intricately crossed, chin down against his chest. In the mixed light from the bedraggled bridge lamp and that from the silver-to-black sky, his thin face, legs, and arms looked luminous and spidery. He seemed like a handsome, pale spider intent on its own web.

"Well, doesn't anyone have any ideas?" Patrick said finally. "She'll be up with the food before long."

"Ideas?" Sylvie challenged. "Like what?" She stared at him, her chin lofty. "All you said was that it was time for us to take some action."

There was attack in her voice. Patrick, sturdy though he was in body and courage, flinched. It was true that he had called for action but had in no way suggested what the action might be. For he did not know. He felt capable of leading the group through whatever trials might beset them, but beyond that his imagination failed.

"All I meant was . . ." Patrick struggled to find the

right words. He had never been articulate. It was because his emotions were so strong, he believed, and because he was primarily a person who liked action first, explanations second. "What I meant was that we don't seem to be getting anywhere just studying bones and skins and planting terrariums and things like that. Especially if there are some live things still out there—besides the wild dogs, I mean." He waved his hand vaguely in the direction of the treeless mountains.

Fay sat straddling an ancient rocking horse that had long ago lost its ability to rock, but often she clucked her tongue at it and gripped its fraying reins as if it were Pegasus with straining wings. She nibbled at a finger nail and said in a half whisper, "I think we should wait and see what Aunt Zeb says." She seemed afraid of her own voice and she was always waiting for somebody else to lead the way. Furthermore, she was too fat. In search of any ally, she turned toward the figure of Knobs crouched over her jacks. "Don't you think so, Knobby?"

*Tap-thud-and-clack. Clack-thud-and-tap.*

Patrick let his breath out through his teeth. They were broad, strong, very white teeth that could chomp an apple in two with one bite. He brushed them faithfully with the electric brush, in fear of decay, having seen his father's yellowing teeth drop out one by one. His legs were fine and strong too but he had never won a race on the track team. He was meant for long-distance running, he believed, and weekly tested himself against the desert slopes around the City, clocking his time and endurance. One thing he knew: he could survive almost any physical test, if it came to that. But could the others? He studied Fay's pudgy arms and legs and felt gloom. Lester? Lester could be a fast sprinter but Lester did not go out for sports.

"Why don't we just wait and see what *she* says?" Fay repeated. Her dark, lustrous eyes were not unlike the sad though false eyes of the oryx.

Lester unwound himself from his yoga-inspired position and lifted his head. His eyes had an amber quality, like those of the lion's head above the card table that served as the Nature Squad's desk. The lion was faded and moth-eaten. In spite of that, there was still a regal air to the maned head, and for all the fierceness of the open, fanged mouth it seemed deeply innocent, terribly betrayed. Just below the shaggy head, suspended from nails that seemed to have been pounded into the wall for no purpose, were spider webs. The spiders that had spun the delicate floss had disappeared long ago, together with ordinary house-flies, moths, snails, and even ants.

"The silver architecture of the past," Aunt Zeb would expound, pointing a strong, big-knuckled finger at the webs. "The delicate artifact of a vanquished species. Walk—and breathe—with care, my darlings."

Lester gazed toward the one window that looked over the garish streets below, the blatant billboards, the sheen and rustle of traffic. "I think that we should go," he said firmly although his changing voice cracked on the last syllable.

"Where?" Patrick said.

Lester kept staring at the window, his amber eyes changing to gray-gold as a green traffic signal below added its color to the room. His upper lip was delicate, quivering slightly above a sturdy lower lip. The color of his eyes changed again under the stabbing reflection of a helicopter's lights glancing off the rooftop of MORTY'S FUN MINT.

"Go where?" Patrick prompted.

"To where the animals are."

Patrick felt a thrill down his spine. It was what he had wanted Lester, or somebody, to say. It was what he had meant to say—or so it seemed now—but he had fumbled all around the idea. Now that Lester had expressed it so simply, he recognized it as exactly what he had wanted to propose. But because of his position of responsibility— and his vision of the four of them heading out into the unknown, the fierce rocks and the moon-splashed peaks, the desolate, poison-riddled spaces abandoned by man and beast—he was forced to throttle his own wild wish to agree at once.

"We don't know where they are—or *if* they are, Les. Do we?"

"Zeb knows!" Sylvie said, her voice ringing, letting the breath out through her nostrils in an expression of impatience with his doubt and caution. There was a yearning light in her eyes. "There could even be butterflies yet —somewhere."

The sound of the jacks and the rubber ball stopped suddenly, noticed at once because it left only the less rhythmic tap and clack of the rain. "I'll go! There's more than butterflies!" There was such enthusiasm in Knobs's normally hollow voice that they all looked toward her. Aside from the fact that she was only eight years old and should not really have been a member of the squad at all, and was therefore treated with forbearance, it was startling for her to voice any opinion. She was a hanger-on, a kind of wan, spindly, knob-kneed ghost with hair the color of dandelion floss and a little mouth so tightly pressed shut it seemed to have been sewn together.

"She's in her own little prison, loves," Aunt Zeb, who was her legal guardian, always told them when they grew impatient. "She'll find the key some day. Remember what happened, dears."

Knobs was snot-nosed just the same, Patrick thought, looking at her and trying to imagine her being part of the Nature Squad out in the wilderness seeking the animals.

"Allergy," Aunt Zeb had said, but it must be more than that. Anyhow, couldn't she wipe her nose more often? Snot-nose wasn't a very nice thing to think or to say, Patrick criticized himself—and he had called Knobs that to her face once—but it was the truth. Furthermore, he was certain she had a low I.Q. His own was high. So was Sylvie's. They had been tested at the same school and had exchanged their scores, both bragging. He did not know about Lester, or about Fay.

Looking at Fay astride the dead rocking horse, he envisioned his struggle across searing rock or sand, bearing Fay's hot weight on his back. No, it wouldn't work. The first duty of a leader on an expedition was to choose his co-explorers with a cold eye toward their qualifications. Sylvie would do; she was agile and bright and determined. Lester would be all right at the start, but he was a sprinter. Knobs? She would be bouncing her jack ball over and over, even as thirst or starvation threatened them all.

His excitement faded. A chain was only as strong as its weakest link, and already this had two. He remembered the century-ago fatal expedition of Captain Robert Scott to the South Pole, the miscalculations that ended in tragedy; he thought of Captain Cook and his fatal error in permitting the Sandwich Islanders to think he was a god; and of the perilous abort of the recent space flight to Mars. And then he thought of Aunt Zeb—Zebrina Morris Vanderbrook. Zeb would go with them, of course. And Zeb would make the difference. Except for Zeb there would never have been a Nature Squad at all, nor the attic office, the dusty spider webs, the wondrous library with its pictures and drawings of all the incredible wealth of wildlife that had once existed not only in Africa and Asia but even here in America.

"There are still some living, breathing, wandering wild creatures out there," Aunt Zeb preached. "Some poor, wandering mountain lion, some fluttering pigeon, some delicate, hiding coyote. They can't have all gone, my treasures."

"She's loony," Patrick's father said. "She ought to be locked up."

Most adults agreed. That was why the Nature Squad's meetings in the attic were secret.

It troubled Patrick sometimes to think that he was actually a subversive, since he was honest and loyal by nature. But ever since the first day that Aunt Zeb had treated him to ice cream, during his Old City paper-route period, and had taken him to the attic where The Heads were, he had felt committed.

"My late husband killed them all," she had said. "He shot them down in bitter, coldest blood and brought them back to me as trophies I should admire. He had a mustache like a walrus." And she had pointed to the walrus head. "Poor thing," she murmured, and Patrick knew she did not mean Colonel James Vanderbrook.

Patrick stood up from the window seat, facing Lester. "We'll have to think it through," he said. "Sylvie, do you have any thoughts. . ."

There was a minor commotion on the stair landing and they all turned to see Aunt Zeb striding forward, lugging a basket as for a country picnic in one hand, a cooler in the other. Her face was flushed with the exertion of her climb up the steps, her ankles swollen and mottled above bare, stout feet in sandals. Her hair, white, frizzy, and abundant, stood out from her head as if it had been electrified by direct current. She clomped forward, peering through thick glasses that obscured her gray-green eyes, and dropped the cooler with a thump. Patrick heard her panting breath. For an instant his dream of her leadership on a mountain safari faded, then rekindled as her lusty voice and vigorous hands took over. There was earth under her finger nails—proof of faithful gardening—and high color in her cheeks from much labor under the sun.

Sylvie went languidly forward to help her distribute the cold beef sandwiches, pickles, oranges, and chilled lemonade. "I would have come down, Auntie Zeb, but I didn't realize what time it was." Fay, too, sidled near, looking apologetic, eager, and ineffectual. Knobs sat silent, then slowly laid her ball and jacks aside, placing the jacks in one solemn row.

"Your stomachs know the time," Zeb said, "but I spoil you. Yes, I do. But I love to do it— Now eat these remarkable products of the Climatron and geodesic barns." There was a touch of sarcasm in her tone. She shoved food and paper cups at them, and a wad of napkins. "Tell me, what grave decisions have been formed in this sanctum above our gamblers' paradise?" She gestured toward domed New City. "Quick now, let me know."

It was Patrick's job as spokesman to tell her of Lester's proposal. At the conclusion he yielded to cowardice, seeing the deepening frown between her grizzled eyebrows. "It was Les's idea. I didn't say one way or the other. Only I did reckon you'd go along—lead the way."

Aunt Zeb removed her glasses—and the children noticed, as always, how uncertain her gaze was without them. She wiped the lenses carelessly against the bodice of her voluminous gown, replaced the glasses, and stared across at the begrimed, tangled hide of a polar-bear rug spraddled on the floor. "Gracious me," she murmured. "Why, what an idea. My dear children, it's quite beyond imagination! I never dreamed—how could you think of such a fantastic project? Surely, I never intimated—or encouraged—such an expedition. It's quite impossible, my dears. Here's your lemonade now." She poured it into the paper cups with such gusto that the pale-yellow liquid went foaming over the sides. "Come along, Celeste," she prompted Knobs, calling her by her true name as she insisted the others should. In fact, Zeb herself often forgot, using the nickname that Patrick had invented. "You didn't get your cooky, love, and I made them especially for you."

Sylvie regarded Aunt Zeb steadily. In the light from the window the small cleft in her round chin showed. "You told us last week, Auntie Zeb, about the mountain lions."

"They don't like people poking around them—if there are any."

"You said that you heard—some doctor or scientist told you—that there were some still around in the Lost Lakes area. And you said . . ."

"Whatever I said," Aunt Zeb answered impatiently, "I certainly did not say that we should go look for them. What I said was . . ." She laid her sandwich down and gazed morosely at the head of a bison mounted on the wall just over her own head. She looked tired. There were lavender pouches under her eyes. "Oh, I don't know what I said, loves. Let's just be quiet and listen to the rain and imagine that there are robins singing in it."

Patrick leafed through his notebook on the card table. "What Sylvie is referring to—it's right here. This news report from the *Highlife Daily*. Quote: 'Two pilots on a mission beyond the abandoned Las Vegas Test Site yesterday reported seeing what appeared to be a lioness and one or two cubs in the wilderness section of Lost Lakes Reservation. Dr. Nathan Friedman, retired mammalogist from Mountain State College, expressed skepticism. No mountain lions, he said, have been seen in the region for some fifty years, and he doubted that there would be any study made, due to the phasing out of the Wildlife Service.' "

Knobs had moved to a floor cushion at Aunt Zeb's feet. She devoured her sandwich hungrily; she always ate as if she were famished. She gulped down the last of the sandwich, then looked up trustingly at Zeb.

"I want to go where the lions and other things are," she said. "But I want you to go, too."

"Hush, child," Aunt Zeb said. "Sunday, tomorrow, we're going to go through my bird's-egg collection again. Remember, Knobs—Celeste—how beautiful the blue of the robin's egg is?"

Knobs twisted one long, pale lock of hair around her forefinger. "I seen all the eggs before. I want to go see the real things."

"Somebody has to lead the way," Patrick spoke up. He could lead for part of it, he was sure, but not all. He looked toward Aunt Zeb.

Zeb had turned her face away. She was gazing somberly toward the window, her chin as square and her mouth as thin-sad as those of the rhino.

"Dear me, perhaps I've misled you," she said as if to herself. "There are dreams—and there are dreams—among the nightmares. Yes, there could be a lone fox, a desperate hare, a panting whale, even a lion kitten—but it would have to be very far away, my dears, and I am not young. Nor naïve. How good to have the natural rain still fall. Do you hear it, my darlings?"

A siren sliced across her voice, a yelp like that of a mechanical animal.

The shadows of the oryx's antlers branched across Aunt Zeb's face. She brushed her hand over one cheek as if she felt the shadow, then took another small, deliberate bite of her sandwich and said cheerily, "Well now, how about our next geology hike? Patrick, you were to arrange for pickaxes and collection boxes. Is that taken care of?"

"Yes," he said, thinking of the project to hack at and study rock strata. He felt dull and sounded dull, having permitted himself to think of finding in a cave somewhere a living, breathing, heart-beating wild creature that he, Patrick Day, would save from potential hunters. The wildernesses beyond the cities were off limits to hunters but he had heard rumors of poachers seeking game. There had been occasional reports that some wild game still existed, but they had not been verified. Also, only a few wilderness places were considered safe for the general public because of the threat of still-existing contamination. Zeb had maintained that there would be no risk in the higher mountains.

Lester was squatted on the polar bear's skin. His thin fingers dragged through its coarse, gray-white pelt. "I may go all by myself," he said.

"Where?" Fay asked, back astride her crippled horse.

"Where the animals are, of course."

# CHAPTER 2

ZEBRINA Vanderbrook could not sleep, not even with the rare and somnolent sound of early June rain beating softly against the bedroom windows. She wrenched and turned, twisting the sheets and light blanket each time until they and her floral-printed nightgown were so entangled that the oversized bed seemed to have been visited by some natural disaster.

"Sleep!" she commanded herself in her firmest undertone, being careful not to wake Knobs in the next room. Eyes squeezed shut, she went through the relaxing routine she practiced at moments of desperation, and these were frequent. My toes are relaxed, my knees are relaxed, my thighs are relaxed . . . The body must be obedient to one's wishes. If not, one ended up catering to a tyrant. She should not, for instance, have eaten so many cookies. If she did not lose weight soon, Dr. Beam would become disgusted and might even refuse to treat all the various ills her flesh was heir to. But the cookies had been extra-delicious, she thought with pride in her own handiwork. And the children had stuffed themselves like the precious gluttons they were.

She wheeled over in bed again, resolutely returning to her exercise in self-hypnosis: hips relaxed, viscera, arms, elbows. . . .

How had the children thought up such a wild idea? Where the animals were, indeed! It was Lester, of course. He had always had too much imagination, inventing dream worlds that had never existed, attributing mystic spirits to pebbles and mud puddles, and stubbornly reading books far over his head, Schopenhauer or Spinoza in one hand, a dictionary in the other. It was a wonderful, dear head, though, she must admit, and she loved watching him, the way he moved like a two-legged cat, and his long hands carefully stroking the birds' eggs or just handling a piece of quartz.

Patrick, too, of course, in his sturdy, dependable way, his cheeks as red as her favorite geraniums. Chester—her long-lost Chester—would have been more like Patrick, active and strong and generous. But he would have had his head swimming with poetry and would have thought deeply like Lester. Ah, but she did not want to think of little Chester. She would think of the living instead, of sweet, shy, chubby Fay, and valiant Sylvie, and uncertain Knobs. They were beautiful children, all of them, but still, a preposterous idea like that—such a journey in summer when the desert would be hot enough to fry bacon on a rock. Of course, once up in the mountains, eight thousand feet or more, it would be cool, even cold. If they could reach there. They would have to carry warm sleeping bags. . . .

Bacon. The thought of it frying, the smoke rising above the tops of cedar and pine, up in the chill, clear mountain morning, made her feel almost faint with hunger and longing. How beautiful it had all been once, years past, before the disasters of misapplied technology. But surely it would be safe up there now after the years of abandonment. Dr. Beam's reports, from his last venture, had been very reassuring. But did she have the strength left to make the attempt? Drat her high blood pressure, her treacherous and ungrateful arteries and veins plotting against her, denying her the simplest of pleasures! Was she supposed to spend all her final years on earth eating grass to avoid cholesterol in her blood stream? Man was not meant to be a vegetarian. He was essentially carnivorous. The comparatively short length of his intestines, like those of the tiger, proved that.

Sleep. She must sleep. I am terribly, utterly relaxed, she told herself. Limp. Sinking. Sliding. A stone falling through water. I am absolutely *unable* to keep awake.

Strange that Knobs—Celeste—should have seized on the idea of the journey so eagerly. Poor little tyke, always hanging around underfoot when she wasn't playing with her jacks, scared of her own shadow, almost afraid to get a jacket or a dress out of the closet for fear some goblin lurking there might clutch her. Almost a ruin of a child she was, as who wouldn't be if her own mother left her hanging on a freeway fence only inches from murderous cars? Zeb sighed. It was not a good thing to think about, especially in the middle of the night.

She turned over again, dragging half the bedclothes with her. She must concentrate on the music of the rain. How heavenly it was after the dry, heat-throbbing days. Or recite a poem to herself. Yes, that often helped.

*Lo! in the mute, mid wilderness,*
*What wondrous Creature?—of no kind!—*
*His burning lair doth largely press,—*
*Gaze fixed, and feeding on the wind?*

Memory failed, jumped, reclaimed another line of the poem.

*From his stately forehead springs,*
*Piercing to heaven, a radiant horn. . . .*

Zebrina sighed, surprised that even that much of Darley's poem, memorized in long-ago college days, remained with her. No one had ever seen a unicorn, the poet said. But people had once seen grizzlies, wolves, and condors. Another hundred years and such creatures, like the unicorn, would seem only mythical. *Feeding on the wind.* "Wind" with a long "i," she reflected, to rhyme with "kind." Wind should always be pronounced that way. Shortening the "i" sound took the soul out of the word.

But what was she doing, fretting about pronunciation at a time like this? Something rattled on the roof and her heart leaped, foolishly, for it was only a guy wire which had fallen the day before and which she had forgotten to ask Patrick to mend. She remembered bright raccoons on her roof in days past, or scuttling to her door at dusk. It hurt to recall how she had struggled against the wily beasts' invading her garden. Red pepper to make them sneeze, poor little innocent bandits—not that that had stopped them. They had always outwitted her, forcing her to laugh in spite of their depredations. Oh, those delicate handlike paws, those dark masks and merry eyes. She thought of the small cork gun she had fired at squirrels to protect her bird feeder. She had avoided hitting them but still she felt remorse. The very sight of a squirrel would be paradise regained. And the hummingbirds that had buzzed around her bottle of sugar water, flashing like pieces of flame wrapped in iridescent green silk.

> . . . *close the Serpent sly*
> *Insinuating, wove with Gordian twine*
> *His braided train, and of his fatal guile*
> *Gave proof unheeded . . .*

*Paradise Lost,* indeed. The pesticides, the oil spills, the nuclear wastes, defoliation, destruction, erosion, war, the great elephants of Asia even ceasing to mate under the furor of the guns. . . . She kneaded her pillow, burrowing her head into it, just as Knobs screamed.

Zebrina bolted up to a sitting position and wrestled free from the coils of the bedding. She groped for her glasses on the bedstand, then ran slap-footed toward the night-light glow of the next room, crying out, "It's all right, Knobby, love. You're only dreaming. Auntie Zeb is here. Wake up, wake up, treasure!"

Knobs was up on one elbow, hunched back against the wall, her eyes wide open but sightless while the screams poured from her throat. Mavis, the tiger-striped kitten, had leaped from its nest beside her and was peering out, terrified, from under the dresser.

"Now, now, now, love," Zebrina crooned, gathering the child against her full, hot bosom. She stroked Knobs's dandelion-floss-colored hair, rocking back and forth like a large, living cradle. "There, there, nothing's going to hurt you. Look now, you've frightened the kitten. See, you're awake, safe and sound in your own room."

Realization and relief swam into Knobs's pale-blue eyes, though a shape of horror still distorted her mouth.

"It was the bad dream again, wasn't it, love?" Zebrina asked. The dream of falling from the roaring fence where Knobs had clung for almost an hour before anyone had noticed or bothered to stop. "Was that it, honey?"

Knobs shook her head and closed her eyes, and Zeb lowered her to the pillow again. "No, it was somethin' else," she murmured. "About the animals." She sighed deeply and slept.

Zebrina went back to her room, draped a brilliantly flowered bathrobe over her shoulders, and pushed her feet into fleece-lined slippers. Shielding the light of her Forever-flash with her hand, she went as quietly as possible back through Knobs's room. The kitten leaped at the opportunity of the opened door and raced down the stairs ahead of her.

A glass of hot milk, Zebrina thought. Or, better, a nip of port. What Dr. Beam didn't know wouldn't hurt him. At her approach the Irish setter, Irene, and the Boston bull terrier, Pepper, both trotted forward, claws clicking against the vinyl of the kitchen floor. Only one of the three adult cats stirred, and that one only to yawn from the couch by the fireplace in the adjoining room. The canary in its covered cage was still.

"Shh-h-h!" she admonished the joyous dogs even as she inspected their empty dishes and went toward the cupboard where their dry food was stored. She filled their dishes, though they were not entitled to more food until morning, and only then reached into the cabinet where a bottle of wine stood, its lean sides dusty. With a small glass of the liquid that glowed like an overripe plum in the fluorescent light from the electric stove, she sat down heavily in the little dinette beneath a rain-streaked window. The stove clock said that it was three hours past her usual ten o'clock bedtime.

She sipped the wine slowly, savoring the forbidden sweet. Even a few drops brought a flush to her face. She felt her cheeks begin to burn. What matter, if it would make her drowsy? Irene pushed her rust-red head against Zebrina's knees. She patted the dog absently, and then the Boston bull in turn. Max, the biggest of the cats, roused himself from his couch and approached the doorway, giving a faint chirp that was astonishingly birdlike. He was a reincarnated sparrow, Zeb jokingly maintained, and a big, fluffy, golden dear, whatever he had been in a former life.

Amazing how stubborn the sparrows were, she reflected. They could still be seen sometimes around the City. And the starlings. It was ironic that foreign imports had managed to endure while the native species had sickened and died. Carp could tolerate an amazing amount of muck in river and pond, but not even they could survive in the utterly dead lakes and rivers. She mourned for the brilliant-bellied sunfish, the leaping trout, and the stout-hearted salmon that had once persisted toward their spawning grounds in spite of the stark, gum-colored, concrete dams in their way. Gone like the kingfisher, the eagle . . .

There was a sound above and she tensed, fearing that Knobs's nightmare had returned. But it was only the loose guy wire rattling again. A dream of animals, Knobs had said. Strange. Perhaps she had been wrong to let the child join the others up there in the attic with The Heads. She should have had The Heads destroyed long ago, for they were gruesome even to her. Taxidermy revolted her—the terrible stuffed owls and coyotes staring from their pedestals in the museums, the deer hunters' prize antlers mounted like dead branches in the now-moldering quarters of vanished sportsmen's clubs. She preserved the mementos partly to keep her anger alive, and to preserve some ghost of the animals themselves. They were Exhibit A in her catalogue of man's crimes against nature.

To be consistent she should have the heads of vanished races there too—bushman, pygmy, Australian aborigine—she thought with unusual bitterness. Perhaps the wine was making her morbid. She set the glass aside, thinking again of Knobs. The child had never truly been out of the City, or any city, except on the grim freeways and on the nearby nature walks and expeditions Zebrina had chaperoned.

Nature could heal, Zebrina mused. Even such nature as was left. There would be no condors gliding over the Lost Lakes area, their black shoulders riding the air currents. And no eagles. How stubborn Lester had been about climbing to that abandoned eagle's nest last year, pitching breath and limb against the dizzying cliff in spite of her pleas and threats. Up and up he had gone, the spidery legs and hands gripping every knob and crevice. Once he had set his mind on a goal, there was no dissuading him. And now the fanatic dream of the trek to "where the animals are."

She could not let him and the others go alone. Even

though she had maintained her belief that in the more remote areas there was a chance that nature had survived man's blind encroachment, she had no proof. The government had made no explorations for years. Even scientists were indifferent, for the world was space-mad. It was as if the entire human species was intent on deserting its earth home for another, cooping themselves up in their sterile domed cities in the meanwhile. And yet suppose that out there, somewhere, birds still sang and foxes hunted? Others, especially of her generation, must have the same thoughts. Dr. Beam, of course. But the rest were either too weak or too timid, clinging to their electronic comforts, fearful of the risk.

No, it was not the risk. It was indifference. People no longer cared to explore beyond the certified-safe boundaries of a community park, or a government-approved hiking party on the "outside." Very few even bothered to go to the few wilderness spots that were sanctioned. But here she had eager youngsters whom she had infected with her own devotion to a different kind of world.

The old clock in the living room struck the half hour, reverberating through the rain-splashed house. Yes, she had indoctrinated them all during the hikes and walks, the boat trips on the tame reservoir lake, the amateur archeological expeditions, the sunrise searches for the sight of one robin or meadow lark, the breathless quest for wild-animal tracks at what had once been an open city dump— while keeping a sharp eye out for fierce feral dogs. How fanatical she had been, reasoning that shy, wild creatures, deprived of their natural forage by the bulldozer, strip mining, and leisure-world developments, might dare to approach the spoilage that still accumulated on the dump grounds in spite of all sanitation laws. The Nature Squad had, of course, found nothing.

But in the mountains? Suppose, as the pilots said, there was a lioness there, and a cub or two? Zeb rested her forehead against her hands, running her fingers through her wild white hair. It was a mirage, a vain hope, like that of the people who in 1914, nearly one hundred years ago, when the last passenger pigeon was dying in its cage in Cincinnati, kept imagining that they saw other passenger pigeons with whom the female bird could mate and so perpetuate the species.

To lead an adventure such as Lester proposed would mark her as mad, as she knew most of her neighbors thought her to be. Who would care for her dogs and cats and the canary? Or her garden? Steve Thorson next door, of course. He had done it before when she had needed to be away. He had been the first member of her Nature Squad when he had been only eleven. He was still a member in her heart even though he had grown beyond her. Steve was studying to become a veterinarian, as he had long dreamed, but now his interests were concentrated on the uses of laboratory animals in space. Even so, he had a persisting attachment to earth-bound creatures, and the vast number of domestic pets, from dogs to hamsters, promised a lucrative practice. Soon he would obtain his degree. With his father killed in the last war and his mother ill, his struggle had been hard, even with Zeb's help. It was easy enough to understand why his interest had been lured by the space program so lavishly subsidized by the federal government.

"Once you are a full-fledged veterinarian," she had joked when they had discussed his eventual degree, "perhaps I should be your first patient. My grandfather was a lone wolf, I'm sure."

"Fleas aren't always simple to eradicate," he had responded, laughing, his red head bobbing sideways as he pretended to duck an expected slap.

Yes, Steve would faithfully care for her animal babies, as she called them, although the setter was beginning to ache with age, and Max Cat had suffered a mild stroke.

"We're all growing old," she murmured, patting the insistent setter's head. Too old to go marching off on a search for the Fountain of Youth, the Cities of Gold, a famished, rib-sided coyote or an unimaginable fawn or a golden lion cub. And to what end? To see them. Perhaps to touch a dappled coat, to hold out a branch or crumb of food, to feel a rough tongue lick one's human palm. But they could not be brought back to panic and die or to end up as zoo specimens. That the children must understand completely. This was not to be a rescue mission— providing there was something to be rescued. Such an undertaking would be too vast, beyond her powers. This would be only to look, perhaps to have a breathless glimpse of a world most people had dismissed or forgotten.

Six of us, she thought. The old station wagon would easily accommodate that many. Food. Gear. Sleeping quarters. The camp trailer with its ample tent expansion would manage her, Knobs, Sylvie, and Fay nicely. The boys could have the nine-by-twelve umbrella tent.

The clock struck two. Go to bed, you old fool, she commanded herself. She switched off the stove light, gave

Irene, Pepper, and Max their final pats and endearments, then followed the flashlight beam back up the stairs. She paused at the bedroom landing, bowed her head and closed her eyes, listening to the blessed rain, and then ascended the stairs to the attic. For it was there, in the filing cabinet her husband had used, that all her maps were.

Maps, she had often thought, were among the most important things in life. For travelers. Was she a traveler —she, white-haired and giddy old woman that she was? She paused midway. Of course! She had always been a traveler. Out there and—she pressed her hand to her chest —and in here. The steps seemed less steep suddenly, her breathing easier.

It's the wine, she reflected, as she neared the top, trying to avoid the creak of old wood under her sheepskin-shod feet. It's gone to my head. In the morning I'll return to sanity. But since I can't sleep, I may as well study the route.

She felt an almost gay enchantment as she sat down at the card table and unfolded the creased maps. Patrick had left his ball-point pen lying on the table. She took it and peered at a map, groaning for lack of her magnifying glass in the room below. Still, the mountains and rivers, deserts and lakes, were printed on her brain. How often in her marriage she had been forced to go with James on his fierce hunting expeditions. How often she had seen the bloody pronghorns, elk, and deer strapped to the car's hood. He had even persuaded her to try her luck once on a hill of gophers.

One bloodied little creature she had struck still tumbled in her memory.

"Sentimentality, my dear," James had derided her expressions of dismay. "Maudlin, utterly."

The tusks of an elephant gleamed dully in the lamplight, protruding from a varnished wall plaque. Squinting beneath their yellowed ivory, frowning, tumbling her hair with her knotty fingers, Zebrina Morris Vanderbrook studied the map and drew the pen across the printed landscape, noting campsites, water holes, elevations, and possible roads.

At three o'clock she slept, her head down across the Lost Lakes, the high Sierra, half of Nevada and Utah, the tip of one large ear butting into the Pacific Ocean.

# CHAPTER 3

THE jacks, each painted a different color, had names, and Knobs always put them in an orderly row in their box when she told them good night. The blue one was Bobby, the red was Rose, the green was Gary, the yellow one was Yerda, the black was Barbara, the white one William. The purple one was Mommy because Knobs seemed to remember that her mother had deep-purple eyes. Mommy had her own special place in the box, way off from all the other jacks. The one jack Knobs never touched was a silver one named Silver Daddy. It stayed by itself in a small cardboard box.

Silver Daddy was real and he was in jail. Aunt Zeb had told her that. It was Silver Daddy who had pushed her out of the car and said, "Hang on to the freeway fence, kid, or you'll get kilt." Mommy had cried out of her deep-purple eyes, and then the car whooshed off and Knobs hung up against the fence, feeling the wind of the other cars, gripping the hard wire with her hands, waiting for them to come back. Only they hadn't, because Silver Daddy wanted to get rid of her. "Just another big mouth to feed," he had kept saying. He wasn't really her father. Nobody was that she could remember. But Mommy was really her mother, wherever she had gone.

"Don't worry, love," Aunt Zeb always said. "You have me now. You'll always have me."

One of the nicest things about Aunt Zeb's house, even though Sylvie had told her it was terribly old, was the big living room with its hardwood floor. It was perfect for playing jacks, smooth and glossy and firm. The small rubber ball bounced as if it had springs in it, and it was easy to scoop up Bobby, Rose, Gary, Yerda, Barbara, and William off the slick surface. She had had the jacks and ball in her dress pocket when the policemen lifted her down from the freeway fence and the jacks had the same names then as now because they were her secret and special friends.

Now, of course, there were Patrick and Lester, Sylvie and Fay.

"They're your real friends, sweet," Aunt Zeb told her.

Maybe. It was hard to know. Knobs bounced the ball against the sunlit floor, hearing Aunt Zeb tramp up from the basement. The jacks, and Aunt Zeb, you could trust and believe in. And the animals in the green book on the shelf where Aunt Zeb kept the books that she called her faithful companions. The books were for grownups and most of them were dull, without any pictures, but the green book was filled with pictures of strange animals. Some were frightening but some were beautiful, and they had names that were hard to read. One of the prettiest was a horse with wings. He was called Pegasus, Aunt Zeb said. One of the other beautiful creatures was a horse, too, with a horn growing out of his forehead.

"That's a unicorn, dear," Aunt Zeb had told her. "Like Pegasus and centaurs and dragons, he's a purely mythical creature. That is to say, they never really existed."

They existed in the book just the same, Knobs thought. And they must have been real, or how could there be pictures of them?

She tossed the rubber ball high, swept up all six jacks, and caught the ball before it touched the floor. That was the hardest of all to do, and she felt triumph, glancing toward the Mommy jack off by itself, and the box that held Silver Daddy. She hadn't dreamed about them and the slot machines for a long while now—the slot machines clanking and flashing and marching in rows through her nightmares. Three nights ago she had dreamed about the Unicorn. He had been the color of moonlight, his single horn glowing, and he had been attacked by a horde of nameless, faceless, shaggy animals. Then suddenly his beautiful head was up on the attic wall, right between the ugly rhinoceros and the elephant, and next she was screaming and Aunt Zeb was holding her.

"Oh, dear!" Aunt Zeb's voice came now from the basement stairway landing. "The mice chewed up this sleeping bag years ago. It had to be years ago, since I haven't seen one of the little gluttons for—well, certainly since the turn of the century. It will have to be patched, that's all there is to it. As for these air mattresses—Celeste, love, could you lend a helping hand?" Under one arm she clutched several sagging plastic air mattresses, while she held the chewed sleeping bag in the other. "See this round valve here in the corner, treasure? You just blow into it and it fills up with your breath. That's what we're going to sleep on."

Knobs stared at the unfamiliar object, then reluctantly arranged her jacks in their proper order and stood up. "Aren't we going to sleep in our beds any more?"

Aunt Zeb laughed. "Out there?" she said, gesturing in the direction of the high mountains that rose steeply to the west of the City. "No, no, dear. We'll have to pack everything with us. Beds. Food. Water. I suppose I should be glad that James had all this camping equipment—it's almost impossible to come by now—even though he and his friends used it for hunting treks and, thereby, destruction. Here, love, just take the valve stem in your mouth and blow. When you need to rest you push the valve down and that prevents the air from leaking out. Unless, of course, there are leaks in the seams." By way of demonstration she began puffing vigorously at the valve of one mattress while she handed Knobs the other.

Out There, Knobs thought, her forehead puckering under her straight, yellow-white bangs. Out There was where the animals were, Lester had said. He and the others had talked about mountain lions and foxes and rabbits. Maybe they didn't know about Pegasus and the Unicorn. Or if they did, perhaps they, like Aunt Zeb, didn't believe in them.

Knobs stood with the air mattress in her hands, most of it dragging on the floor, and pressed her mouth around the plastic valve. The beautiful creatures could be Out There, no matter what anybody thought. Even Aunt Zeb could be wrong. Three days ago, with the rain falling, she had thought about searching for Pegasus and yearned to go. But she had lost hope when Aunt Zeb had declared the whole idea was impossible.

Now she felt a rush of excitement. I'll die if we don't go, she thought, her breath sputtering around the valve.

"I would absolutely never have considered this," Aunt Zeb said, holding down the shut-off valve on her own mattress with a heavy thumb, "except for their audacity. First Lester, and then Patrick, scheming to take off without me. They would have done it, too, Celeste, if I hadn't surprised them in their preparations. They would have romped off without adequate gear or knowledge of the terrain. It's partly my fault I know, having talked too much about what might be out there—but to think of those innocents marching out into the unknown with no proper guide! What else can we do, love, but go with them? They would assuredly have talked Sylvie and Fay into it too. Sylvie, indeed, would have insisted.

"What I think, Knobs—Celeste—is that we can hold it to a safe two or three days' outing, and that will take care of it. Isn't that right, dear? We'll just try to find some nice mountain meadows with shade, where it's safe, and camp a bit, then return without any fanfare. It'll be good for all of us. Especially you, treasure." Perspiration trickled down from the widow's peak of her hairline, and in the light from the windows the mole on her large right ear gleamed like a brown earring. She raised the valve of the air mattress to her mouth once more, pursed her lips, then unpursed them. "We won't really find anything out there, you know. Or at least it's most unlikely. Oh, dear, I shouldn't have gotten their hopes up."

*Whoosh-whoosh-whoosh* she blew into the air valve, her white hair in an uproar above her determined head.

There was no need to answer, Knobs knew, as she puffed

air into her own mattress. Aunt Zeb was mostly talking to
herself, and she could do this for minutes at a time, not
expecting anybody to talk back. Though, once in awhile,
she would demand impatiently, "Knobs, are you listening?
Say something, child!"

For the moment there was only the heavy breathing of
both of them as they sighed and puffed over the slowly
inflating mattresses. From the kitchen came the sudden
song notes of the caged canary, and Knobs stopped blowing in order to listen. Years ago, Aunt Zeb said, there had
been wild, free birds who sang outside with similar voices.
Now almost the only way to have such music was to have
it in a cage.

"Perhaps it's cruel," Aunt Zeb had said once. "Some
people think so. But if it's a case of imprisoned singers or
none . . . Oh, I don't know, Knobs. But I don't think
Goldie minds the cage. And think of all the baby songsters
I once raised and gave away. A whole feathered symphony,
love. They'd die if they were freed. When I think about
all the wrens and robins that dashed themselves against
the dome of New City— Well, I won't think about it,
and that's final!"

Knobs studied the air mattress, seeing it swell with her
own breath. It was odd to think about sleeping on air that
came out of a person's own lungs. She paused, pushing the
valve down as Aunt Zeb had instructed, resting, disturbed
by doubt, but saying nothing. There wouldn't really be
anything Out There, Zeb had said; like playing the slot
machines and getting nothing back, or at least much less
than you put in.

Night after night, Mommy and Silver Daddy had taken

her with them to the casinos, and she had sat in a chair waiting and waiting for them to leave the machines and go home. Sometimes it went on all night and she would fall asleep, or half asleep, with the machines clanking and flashing, the sounds of dimes and dollars clattering down through a chute, the flap of cards at the blackjack table, the purr of the roulette wheel, and the rattle of dice.

Aunt Zeb was blowing up her mattress again. Knobs said to her, "There could be things we don't know about."

Aunt Zeb looked up, her cheeks still puffed out. "Things —where—what do you mean, honey?"

"You said we wouldn't really find anything." There was a quaver in Knobs's voice.

Zeb lowered her heavy glasses and gazed over them, seeming to look into far distances though Knobs knew that she was almost blind without the glasses. "Did I say that, precious? Well, I only meant we mustn't count on too much. It's mostly to be a brief camping trip, for the fun and adventure of it, you know." She lowered her chin against her ample chest and rubbed one garden-callused hand against her mouth, murmuring to herself, "Though, per- haps, I should take James's old .22— Well, never mind, dearest. Why, your mattress is blown up already. That's wonderful! You're 'way ahead of me; I've been blabbing too much. Now, we'll let them lie right here and see if they leak—heaven forbid!—though I do have that marvel- ous plastic-sealing compound. Let's see—six mattresses and bags, and dehydrated food. Canteens. No problem with those, or compass. Knapsacks and . . ." She gave several final vigorous puffs at her mattress and laid it be- side Knobs's before looking off to the blue shadows of the

mountains soaring behind New City's bubble canopy.
"There could be some wild flowers yet, blooming about
now. If you could have seen the lupine once, dear heart,
acres of it, yellow and blue and lavender bushes like big
flowering cushions, and the hummingbirds going in and
out like little comets, and the fields of poppies. Douglas
iris, too, and Indian warrior, and sheets of forget-me-nots.
Which reminds me, did you water the pansies this morning, and the begonias?"

Knobs studied the floor. "I forgot. I only did the lemon
tree."

"But that doesn't need watering yet, darling. You can
kill it with too much."

Knobs nodded, feeling guilty. It was the lemon tree in
its brilliantly painted planter that was her favorite.

"You can love things to death."

Knobs nodded again, turning to go to the porch garden
where the flowers and watering can were. If she ever found
a baby Unicorn, or a baby Pegasus, maybe she would love
it to death, even though it didn't seem possible that love
would do that. Once she had almost hugged Mavis the
kitten to death, though, until Aunt Zeb stopped her. Now
Knobs was very careful. She would be careful with the baby
animals Out There, too, she told herself. She would
scratch the Unicorn's forehead so lightly he would hardly
feel it, and only touch the flying horse's wings with one
finger. One thing, she would never tell the others about
her find. It would be her special secret, like the names of
the jacks. Otherwise, people would laugh. Maybe Fay
wouldn't. She liked Fay the best. But Patrick was nice too,
even though he had called her Snot-nose once.

Not that they mattered too much as long as Aunt Zeb was there. Aunt Zeb could take care of anything and she would never let anybody be hurt.

Knobs picked up the watering can and pushed her nose into the blossoming lemon tree, breathing in. Next time I blow up the mattress, she thought, I'll breathe in the lemon blossoms first and then I'll be sleeping on lemon-tree smell. Out There, under the stars.

If we don't go, I'll die.

But they would go, she knew they would. And she would take Bobby, Rose, Gary, Yerda, Barbara, and William with her. That way there would always be company. Mommy could go too, she decided. And Silver Daddy, but only in his separate box.

The pansy blossoms seemed to have tiny faces looking up at her. She sprinkled the water over them very carefully, then heard the snarl below. Knobs looked over the railing of the high porch supported by tall piers. The neighbor's greyhounds were having a fight, three of them racing after the runt of the litter, who went squealing off in panic. There was big money in greyhound racing, Aunt Zeb had told her. Every day the slim, lean-haunched dogs raced around the circular training track in pursuit of a mechanical rabbit.

A real rabbit, Knobs thought, would be soft, like a kitten. There could be rabbits Out There. It wouldn't be the same as Pegasus or the Unicorn but it would be something to find.

Aunt Zeb's Irish setter and the Boston terrier came trotting toward her. She patted them timidly, then remembered Patrick's mention of wild-dog bands Out There, and shivered in spite of the hot sunshine.

I'll go anyhow, she determined. Aunt Zeb kept saying that she must learn to be brave.

She gave Irene's rust-brown muzzle an extra stroke, and scratched Pepper a second time between the ears, then set the watering can down, completely forgetting the thirsty begonias.

# CHAPTER 4

NEW City glittered under its steel-and-Plexiglas dome, eternally air-conditioned, forever beyond the reach of rain, snow, or frost. Its lighting system provided for the same amount of illumination daily whether the sun shone or not. However, there was provision agreed on by the Council for certain gray days, as it had been found that continual, unfluctuating light created monotony and affected people's mental states. The dome was soundproof, too, so that the constant air traffic overhead made only the thinnest hum. Once a supersonic transport had wandered off its wilderness flyway and had created a sonic boom of such proportions that almost a quarter of the dome had cracked, and a dozen unprotected houses in Old City had been reduced to rubble. However, that had been a rare accident; the SSTs and the Global Freight Ships ordinarily flew only specified wilderness and ocean routes between the widely scattered population centers.

The people in New City marveled that anyone in his right mind would live outside its protective dome. Only eccentrics or the very poor clung to the unsheltered slopes, and each year the number of those decreased so that the growing population pressure within the dome was intense. There was talk about the need to enlarge the canopy by another hundred square miles.

Of the Nature Squad, only Fay lived outside the dome, not far from Aunt Zeb's house. Her envy of Patrick, Lester, and Sylvie was keen. During the school year she went regularly to New City to school, and each day when she had to board the Turbo-van that took her and other Old City children back to their homes, she felt humiliated. Outwardly, she pretended that she much preferred life under the open sky.

"My mother and father love the wind and the rain," she would declare with desperate boldness to questioning classmates. "And so do I. I'd hate to live all bottled up, without ever hearing the wind or anything."

That part of it was true. Aside from the dome's prestige, and its protection from sonic booms, lightning, and disease germs, she did prefer the natural sounds of wind or rain, and the real sun on her skin. But it was not true that her parents lived where they did out of choice. It was simply that they were too poor to live elsewhere. Daddy, an ordinary maintenance man with the Hovercraft Corporation, had all he could do to support the family where they were now. Fay and her five brothers and sisters rarely saw him except on Sundays—and often not even then—for he was constantly taking on extra jobs. Mother was gone a lot, too, working in New City as a practical nurse.

One of the hardest things of all, Fay thought as she made her way to Aunt Zeb's, was having so many brothers and sisters. Scarcely any families had more than one or two children. It was embarrassing when anybody asked her,

"Do you have a brother or sister?" to have to answer that she had four sisters and a brother.

Even Knobs is better off than I am, Fay brooded, pausing in the shade of the high porch that extended all along one side of Aunt Zeb's house. Though Fay claimed that she liked the feeling of the actual sun on her skin, she glanced back toward New City with a yearning for its unvarying mildness, and envisioned the splash of cooling fountains there, the lush gardens along the sidewalks, flowers bursting out all year from the specially aerated and nourished soil. In contrast, Aunt Zeb's marigolds planted beside the front steps looked scraggly and defeated. The grass was scrubby, too, though it was better than the completely bare ground around her own house.

She was panting from her climb and wondered how she would fare on the trip to the outside. So far, on the short expeditions the Squad had made before, she had managed to keep up well enough in spite of her weight. But the excess pounds were a handicap. It was unfair. She didn't eat any more than her sisters or brother did, but they were all as skinny as Knobs.

Oh, why can't I be slim? she wondered, looking off toward the mountains rearing up from the desert floor. The shadows in their creases were blue and cool-looking but she knew that these were deceptive. It would be a hot journey until the Squad reached the cottonwood creeks and the chaparral and then climbed to the forests. Would there really be any wild animals roaming there? It would be nice if there were, but the important thing was being with the Squad and getting away from all the things she hated about the City, Old or New, and especially her oldest sister, Martha.

"Where are you gadding off to now?" Martha had demanded when Fay left the house. Martha was sixteen and dreamed out loud about being married some day and moving to a "real rich" high-rise in New City. "You're supposed to do the dishes, Chub."

Fay flushed at the hated name. "I'll do them when I come back."

"Back from that crazy old woman's house, I bet. Everybody knows she's crazy."

"She's not!" Fay defended. "She's smart. She's read all kinds of things and she knows everything about nature."

"Nature!" Martha scoffed, a purplish birthmark dark against her thin white neck. "Weeds and sand and rocks. And storms. That's nature." She looked at the scabby yard and a range of bony, desolate-appearing hills to the north with disgust. "I'll take the City, thanks."

"Who's stopping you?" Fay had thrust.

There was a sound of footsteps on the high porch above and Fay looked up to see Knobs with her nose pressed into the lemon tree. "Hi," Fay called.

Knobs jumped, startled, then stared wordlessly down.

"I'm late," Fay said. "Are the others here?"

Knobs nodded.

Fay climbed the steps leading to the porch and stood beside Knobs. From there she could see Patrick's two-seater minibike below. A military aircraft swooped over the distant hills, leaving a long, white contrail behind it. A second later the porch reverberated in response to a distant rumble from the Ultra Target Site. That was one place the Squad could never go. It was terrible, Patrick said. He had flown over it with his father once in a Rent-a-plane from his father's lot.

"It's dead," Patrick had said. "Just completely dead. There wouldn't be a worm alive out there."

Fay realized that Knobs was looking up at her, her pale mouth moving as if she were going to say something. Fay went over and sniffed at the lemon tree, silent, waiting. Sylvie was impatient with Knobs, but that was because Sylvie found it hard to be patient with anyone who wasn't as smart or self-sure as she was. Even though Knobs had not responded much to Fay's attentions, Fay always thought of herself and Knobs as being in league against Sylvie.

"I heard somethin' this morning," Knobs said to Fay's back.

Fay turned. "What, honey?" She tried not to be either too curious or too indifferent.

"A song."

"What kind of song?"

A faint pink touched Knobs's cheekbones, a hint of excitement. "It was in the air, and flyin'. Only it wasn't Goldie. Goldie's in his cage." She lowered her voice to a whisper as if they might be surrounded by spies. "Aunt Zeb heard it too. It was a cañon wren, she said, and it went 'tsee-i' at first and then lower, 'too-ee, too-ee.' I heard it and I ran in and told her, and then we both ran out here and she was so excited she didn't know what to do. I heard it first!" Pride brightened her eyes. Then, as if she had betrayed too much, she turned and ran indoors toward the attic stairway.

Fay followed, wondering just what the wren's song had been like and wishing that she had been in Knobs's place. Aunt Zeb was constantly urging the Squad members to report any unusual bird song if they happened to hear one. But though Fay had listened faithfully whenever she had a chance, she had heard only a few sparrows or screechy starlings. Once, in the night, she thought she had heard an owl, or what she imagined might be an owl. Owls went "Whoo-whoo-whoo" according to an old bird book she had read, but the sound she had heard was nothing like that. Or it had not seemed like it at the time. But in the morning, thinking back, she decided that perhaps the bird or whatever it was had actually been calling out "Whoo-whoo-whoo," and she had reported it to the Nature Squad at the next meeting.

"I heard an owl," she stated, standing up in front of them all, squirming with shyness and the knowledge that she was claiming something she did not know at all for certain. Sylvie had gazed at her with frank disbelief, and Patrick had sat without any expression on his bright-cheeked face. Lester had studied the tip of one of his shoes, almost as if he had not heard. Knobs had been playing with her jacks and had not paid any attention.

Aunt Zeb had said only, "Wouldn't it be marvelous, Fay, if it actually were an owl? In spite of the reports of ornithologists ten years back regarding the presumed extinction of all Strigiformes—the owl family—it is not altogether impossible that they are wrong."

"I mean— I think it maybe was an owl," Fay amended.

"Perhaps you'll hear it again, dear, and can report on it with more certitude. One thing, it proves that we must all keep our eyes and ears open and perhaps may see, as the poet said, 'A World in a Grain of Sand and a Heaven in a Wild Flower, hold Infinity in the palm of your hand and Eternity in an hour.' " Then she had turned quickly to a discussion of rock samples the group had gathered near Rim Mountain.

The owl had never been referred to again, but Fay continued to feel guilty about it, for she had, she knew, half invented the owl's voice. Yet she had heard *something* unusual out in the night. Now, following Knobs toward the attic, she felt that it was unfair that Knobs, who paid so little attention to anything outside herself, should be the one to earn Aunt Zeb's praise and excitement.

Patrick glanced up briefly as Knobs and Fay entered, then concentrated again on sorting out the dehydrated food packages assigned to him. The rest of the Squad were busy fixing up the other supplies—ropes, stakes, canteens, musty sleeping bags, kits, and all the rest of the paraphernalia needed. Sylvie, Fay saw, was fussing with a decrepit butterfly net. As if there would be any butterflies out there! Or if there were, it would be unforgivable to capture one and so reduce the already nearly vanished species.

The rifle was what had surprised Patrick the most. True, he had mentioned the possibility of wild-dog bands, but there had been no mention of them in the news for years now. When he was very little, there had been stories about the dogs, how they had reverted to the wild, living on whatever they could find to eat—sometimes devouring each other, according to the grisly stories. Not that it wasn't wise for Zeb to be prepared.

From the corner of his eye, Patrick had seen Lester

looking toward the gun more than once, for all that Les was supposed to be busy patching leaks in the air mattresses. Lester, Patrick had discovered once to his surprise, knew a good deal about firearms because of his military father. Or so Lester had said. Whatever the truth, Les didn't look too happy about the gun's presence.

"None of you must touch it, darlings," Aunt Zeb had ordered, "even though it's unloaded and has the safety catch on." She herself had handled it gingerly as she stashed it in its place. "I would never keep a loaded gun in my house. Weapons of any kind are an invitation to violence, and I am generally firmly opposed to having them accessible. I resurrected it only because— Well, there is always the possibility of emergencies. I, alone, am to carry it, understand? That's a command, children. It will be mostly a nuisance, of course—but I am responsible to your parents for your safety."

A lot most of the parents cared, Patrick thought, having chiefly his father in mind. Dad was seldom home enough to care about anything except sobering up in order to crawl to the used-plane lot in the mornings. It was much the same for the rest of the kids; Sylvie's folks traveling all over the world giving clavichord-and-flute concerts; Lester's parents separated, and infighting so much when they were briefly together that neither cared much about what happened to Les. Fay was just another digit in her bedlam of a household. And Knobs, of course, was a special case. Anyhow, Aunt Zeb was passing this expedition off as a limited camping trip.

But it wasn't the truth, Patrick surmised. She had hauled together enough food and other supplies to last for at least two weeks. And there was the telltale gun. At first, nobody had noticed it in the excited clamor over the wren Knobs and Zeb had heard.

"I raced indoors for the tape recorder," Aunt Zeb had told them, "but I was too late, even if I knew how to operate the silly machine. But oh, how I wish I could have recorded those sweet and glorious notes so that we could all share them together. Perhaps next time. If there is one wren this close to civilization, so called, must there not be others? Yes, it has to be!"

The ring of Zeb's voice made it seem that it did, indeed, have to be. Only the often-skeptical Sylvie challenged her. "Maybe it's the last one of its kind."

"Dear me, let us hope not," Zeb said. "Now, I'm not one to maintain that every cloud has a silver lining. Yet there isn't any point in seeing only the black side of things either, is there, darling?" She looked at Sylvie quizzically through her strong glasses.

Sylvie shrugged. "I don't know. I guess not. Only— Well, that way you're safer. Then you won't be disappointed."

"It is better to have hope and be disappointed than to have none," Zeb said firmly.

"The important thing," Lester interjected with equal conviction, "is to be a realist."

Patrick grinned. "When you get to be one, Les, let me be the first to know."

There was faint crimson along Lester's high cheekbones, but he smiled and said nothing, going back to his plastic-seal work on the air mattresses. He liked Patrick. They had been neighbors in New City for a long while. But they

seldom saw things in the same way, except for their interest in nature and their mutual hope of discovering that
some forms of animal life might have survived the wars
and environmental destruction. For Patrick it was a practical kind of thing, a necessity for ecological survival.

There was something more than that involved, in Lester's opinion. There was the factor of human responsibility,
as old as Adam. And there was the beauty factor. St. Francis had been well aware of the beauty and innocence of
the animals, and even of the elements. Brother Ass,
Brother Fire. Thinking about the wilderness, Lester saw
himself as a similar mystic able to converse and commune
with the possible creatures that might have survived. Self-
discipline was essential. He struggled for it continually, remembering the words of the *Bhagavad-Gita*. In order to
attain a state of union with Brahma, the eternal spirit of
the universe, it was necessary, the *Gita* said, to shut off
sense "from what is outward, fixing the gaze at the root of
the eyebrows."

Right now he had trouble fixing his gaze on anything,
his soft dark hair hanging in his eyes as he worked on a
leaky seam. Life was full of such incongruities, he reflected,
not knowing whether to be amused or despairing. Man is
a bridge, not a goal, Nietzsche said. Lester's fingers were
increasingly sticky from the plastic glue he was using and
he looked, finally, toward Aunt Zeb for some relief.

She recognized his problem immediately and rushed
forward with a bottle of solvent. "You poor dear—I should
have provided you with this earlier. Knobs, come here.
Start testing the mattress Lester mended last night. Fay,
love, can you untangle that viper's nest of rope in the

corner?" Rubbing one side of her ample nose, Zeb pondered other orders. "Sylvie—please stop fooling with that butterfly net and devote your energies to organizing the cook kits. We are not going to be fed manna, you know."

Zebrina's voice was sharp, as it could be on occasion. Her patience was being tried, her tone said. Sylvie winced, hurt at being singled out for reprimand. It wasn't as if the others were being so dutiful, she grieved. She was tempted to cry except that Zeb had no patience with tears. Sylvie herself didn't either; she had seen her mother weep too often after bad reviews of a concert. But it did hurt, especially, to have Aunt Zeb snap at her. Zeb seldom snapped at Knobs or at Fay.

She likes them better than she does me, Sylvie decided, mechanically assembling the compact aluminum kits of cups, plates, and pans. Nobody likes me. Especially Mother and Father. And the housemother at the school hates me. I hate her, too. And I don't even care if we find any animals —even butterflies—out there. Only if I don't go, I'll be all alone most of the summer with Mrs. Giddings.

Mrs. Giddings was the housekeeper in the large apartment that Sylvie's parents owned. She was kind enough, Sylvie acknowledged, a small and chirping woman who spent all her spare time writing indignant letters to politicians and news-media editors, but it seemed to Sylvie that they both rattled around like prisoners in a big, polished cage complete with grand piano, a vast library of musical scores, magical built-in ovens and deep freezes, wall-wide three-dimensional television, and nothing much else. One thing was certain, Sylvie thought: Mother and Father would not be a bit worried if she left a note saying she was going out with the Nature Squad for a few days or weeks. She had tried once to explain what the Squad was but they had barely listened and said nothing beyond murmuring that she should do whatever was "creative and happiness-making." Mother had added, "As long as it isn't something dangerous." They might not even know about the adventure until she was back, since they were now on an extended tour of Europe. Sylvie tried to remember where they were this week—Brussels, The Hague? Mother was a poor letter writer. What Sylvie usually received were post cards, exaggeratedly colored photographs of glamorous places, with Mother's familiar scrawl saying briefly, "Fabulous place here, and rave reviews. Be good, sweetheart. We miss you. Write. Love and kisses."

At the beginning, Sylvie had struggled to figure out their itinerary and have her carefully printed letters waiting for them at their hotels—printing the words then because she had been only five years old at the time and had not yet mastered script. She had labored to express her loneliness in childish language, her desire to share their lives, even as she tried to reassure them that she was well and happy, in case they were concerned—as she hoped they were.

"Mrs. Giddings has a sore throat, but I haven't caught it. We went to the new Exploratorium yesterday. It was very exciting with lots of knobs and buttons to push, and a plastic robot called Albert. I got five Superior marks on my grades. When will you be home? Love and kisses."

Mother always signed her cards that way, so Sylvie had done the same. But lately Sylvie only signed "Love." It seemed more adult; anyway, there had never really been any kisses, only a kind of brief peck and an absent-minded hug from either Mother or Father.

Years ago, before she was born, Father had had a hobby of hunting butterflies, already rare then. There were several specimens pinned on racks under a glass in the apartment. One was outstandingly beautiful, a rare, brilliant blue swallowtail. This was in a special case all by itself.

"Probably one of the last of its species," her father would explain to guests. "I could sell it to a museum for a fortune."

Sylvie daydreamed about the blue butterfly and saw it in her mind now as the sky beyond the attic window reflected its blue light against the aluminum camp kit in her hands. She realized that Aunt Zeb was leaning over her, one hand placed gently on her head. "You're almost through, aren't you, love? A boring job, too, but life is full of those. However, with your imagination and my camp cookery knowledge, why don't we go downstairs and plan the journey's menus?"

Sylvie leaped up, reassured. Aunt Zeb had chosen her for what was truly important. As she followed Zeb from the attic, she glanced back and saw Fay squatting under the bearded old bison's head, struggling with tangled ropes. There was a wistful look in Fay's dark eyes as she gazed after Aunt Zeb and Sylvie.

Sylvie paused. Poor, fat Fay. Like Knobs, she always seemed to be back in the shadows somewhere, left out. "Fay, why don't you spend the night with me in New City before we go?" she called, somewhat to her own surprise. Fay's finger nails were not always the cleanest, and her parents were apparently horribly poor. More reason, then, for charity, Sylvie told herself. No, not charity. Friendship. They were going on a serious adventure together.

Fay blinked in surprise, then pretended to consider the matter. "I don't know . . ." she began, but her brown eyes were gleaming. "All right. I don't care—if you really mean it."

"I wouldn't have suggested it if I hadn't meant it," Sylvie responded more snippily than she meant. She softened the sharpness with a smile. "Of course I mean it, Fay. Why wouldn't I?"

Knobs was in her corner, playing with her jacks. "Tsee-i," she imitated the cañon wren's song in a soft, whistling undertone. "Too-ee, too-ee."

# CHAPTER 5

IT was barely light. The old station wagon, one of the last automobiles made with an internal-combustion engine, stood gleaming dully in Zebrina Vanderbrook's driveway. Looking at it, the luggage carrier heaped high with camping equipment, and at the tent trailer hitched behind, Zeb had a half-hysterical impulse to laugh even as panic edged her thoughts.

Perhaps she was indeed out of her mind to set out on such expedition. She turned toward Steve Thorson, who was supervising the hitch installed by Patrick, and when he looked toward her and nodded his approval, she felt reassured. He had a clown's upturned mouth, and freckles to match his red hair, but there was a deep, still dignity in him, and a grave seriousness of mind that belied his easygoing manner. She knew that he was not entirely approving of her venture.

He strolled toward her, his space vet's uniform so clean and pressed it seemed to crackle. He held up the duplicate copy of their route map that she had given him. "Maybe the Lost Lakes area where you're heading is fit for human occupancy, but the area around it is doubtful, Aunt Zeb.

Take care, wherever you are. You have all the proper anti-
dotes?"

"Of course," she said, somewhat irritated. "You've let
them brainwash you, dear."

"O.K., O.K.," he said, holding his hands up in a de-
fensive posture. "Anyhow, I'll keep the map under my
pillow. As for the babies"—he chuckled at the use of the
word for Zeb's various pets—"I'll watch over them as if
they were being groomed for the first flight to Jupiter."

"Or as if they were little earth-dwellers I care about?"

"That, too. Great good luck, Zeb. When should I put
out the carpet for your return?"

She hesitated. "No more than seven days, Steve.
Roughly. If we don't find something worth while by then
—well, that should be the limit."

"By 'worth while' you mean wild animals?"

"I do."

Steve shook his head. "Wild dogs, horses, or cats, maybe. But . . ." Though he glanced off toward the mountains, she could see that his vision went far beyond them
to the void of space. Perhaps he was envisioning mythical
animals—space unicorns and celestial dragons.

"All set, Auntie Zeb!" Patrick called out. He had recently received his driver's license and had started the car's
engine, but he had relinquished the driver's seat and was
waiting for her to climb in behind the wheel. He and the
others looked toward her, their faces full of anticipation
and impatience.

"I'll be there in a sec, darlings," she answered above the
steady roar of the old engine. In spite of its age, its anti-
pollution devices were shiny new, something that Zeb

watched zealously. She had on a well-worn safari outfit
which consisted of a knee-length nylon skirt fitted with
pockets of all sorts, sturdy hiking boots, a pedometer
strapped below one knee, and a pith helmet over her white
hair. The helmet was a trifle large, having belonged to
James, and it tended to press her ears down. It was shade,
not style, that mattered, she had decided as she had grimaced at herself in the mirror that morning. Still, the effect
was somewhat ludicrous and she had recklessly, out of a
nearly forgotten vanity, considered abandoning the head-
gear altogether. She would not need either the helmet or
the pedometer for some time but it was simpler to wear
them than to pack them.

"You have your radioactivity meter?" Steve questioned.

"Yes, dear, and all the other cunning little gauges and
meters our scientific geniuses have managed to think up.
Don't worry. I shall be prudent, you may be sure." She
adjusted her glasses, studying him. "You didn't always
think of the wilderness as being so frightening. Remember
when we so daringly went one morning years ago to Death
Gulch? The very name was terrifying then."

"Still is," he said with a smile. "Yes, I remember. I was
scared then, too, even though it was a comparatively non-
toxic area at that time. But it was worth it. I'm only concerned now about you." His gaze went to the car. "And
them. Too bad you don't have a GEM."

A ground-effects machine riding on cushions of air. It
would certainly make travel simpler, she knew, but such
machines were horribly expensive and only municipal transport systems or the military used them. A few were privately
owned, but the private owners would never venture with

them beyond the environs of the glassed-in suburbs and their golf courses. Steve had not meant her to take him seriously, she realized; he knew the limitations of her income.

"With any kind of road at all, we'll make it," she said. "If we do actually find some wild creatures out there, think of the thrill for the Squad—for me—something for them to remember forever, and something to work for in the future. Somebody has to care!"

"We're at the stage," Steve said somberly, "where we may soon be able to create completely new animals—animals with the intelligence and docility to serve man as he dictates."

"Oh, Steve, darling—animal slaves, you mean!" She had lost him to the new science, she feared. And yet his earlier dedication, or what she thought of as dedication, to animal life remained. There was no time for discussion or argument. "We'll be all right," was all she said.

He draped a lean arm around her shoulders and gave her a hug. She planted a swift kiss on his cheek, the excitement of the moment bringing tears to her eyes. She brushed at them impatiently before striding toward the car, calling cheerfully, "Everybody ready? Safety harnesses all fastened?"

"Ready! Ready!" the children cried, Knobs's reedy little voice joining in.

"We're off, then," Aunt Zeb said with exuberance as she put the station wagon into motion, waved at Steve, and sent the car firmly on its way down the driveway toward the empty highway out of Old City. "Good-by-y-y, good-by-y-y, be always kind and true," she sang.

The children joined in, for the scrap of a song was a ritual whenever they set off on a journey or broke camp.

"And hooray-y-y, hooray-y-y!" Patrick continued. "We're on our way-y-y today-y-y. Hey, hey!"

Sylvie and Fay giggled and improvised additional lines of their own. Lester remained silent, aloof, gazing out at the dim landscape with an air of combined anticipation and deep thoughtfulness.

"Come on, Lester, sing," Sylvie coaxed, sitting next to him in the back seat.

He looked apologetic. "With my voice?"

Fay giggled and said to the others, "He used to be a male soprano. Now he's a boy bass." Her attempt at wit brought no immediate response and she wished she had not said anything. It was very hard to know what made some people entertaining and others dull. It was better for her not to try being amusing, for it seldom worked. She and Knobs shared the crowded luggage deck behind the back seat, and Fay wondered if Knobs would attempt to play with her jacks in the small amount of bare space available.

"Boy bass. Written down it would look as if Les is a boy fish," Patrick said from the front seat.

Sylvie made an answering quip and then Zeb cut in to say, "I'd rather have a little silence right now, Squad. Whom did I assign to the medical kit?"

"Me," Lester said. "It's all in order, packed in the corner here where it's handy. The snake kit's there, too."

"Snakes, ugh!" Fay said with a shiver.

"Snakes are a very important part of the ecology," Lester remarked. "And most are harmless."

"Yeah," Patrick said. "Because they're all dead."

"Not necessarily," Sylvie argued. "I read just last week that they had a high survival rate, at least in the zones where the contamination wasn't total."

"But they have to have insects and rodents to feed on," Patrick answered.

"Please," Aunt Zeb said. "We can argue about all that later. Fay, you checked out all the thermo flasks, did you?"

"I counted them three times over," Fay answered. She had, but now she tormented herself for fear she might, somehow, have miscounted or have left one out of the pack. "I think they're all there," she added less certainly.

"I'm sure they are, dear," Aunt Zeb said, looking in the rear-view mirror. The highway was empty except for one long truck-train steaming over a distant slope. The commute from the unsheltered fringes to New City wouldn't begin for an hour or more, she reflected, and by that time they would be on the Starway Road. It had been a magnificent six-lane highway once, a glassphalt serpent for the bumper-to-bumper traffic of all the people who had skied, fished, or hunted in the Lost Lakes and Crystal Crag areas. It had been abandoned now for years except for a daring few, mostly of the older generation like herself, who ventured to explore at lower levels what was left of desert rocks and ghost towns. Government permits had been granted only to those who had proved they knew how to take all precautions and had experience in hiking and camping. Although she still had her yellowing permit, it was no longer of importance. The government had let the whole matter lapse for the simple reason that nobody was interested in obtaining such permits any more.

She had not been on the Starway Road for several years, but the aging Dr. Beam, as devoted to exploration as she until his recent heart attack precluded extra exertions, had told her some months ago that the road was passable for at least one hundred miles, and probably more. "If you don't mind bumps and potholes," he had added. Eventually, she knew, if they ventured far enough, they would have to proceed on foot, as they were prepared to do.

Knobs had her face pressed to the tail-gate window, looking not at the steep mountains ahead but at the road vanishing behind. The road kept narrowing to a black V, seeming to come to a point on the horizon, but she knew that it was actually as wide there as here. It was because of something called perspective, Aunt Zeb had explained. The word didn't make the fact any less strange. She wished she could be sitting up front beside Zeb, but Patrick was Zeb's copilot, as Zeb called him, and was in charge of the maps. He was supposed to take a turn driving, too, if she grew tired.

The children began to chatter again, except for Lester and Knobs. Zebrina ignored them in her concentration on the landscape. Night and day were perfectly balanced for the moment, the gold and the blue pitched against each other. In spite of the ruined and rubble-strewn landscape, she held her breath, intent on the gold rim of the sky in the rear-view mirror, the rim of blue ahead, the mountains looking like paper cutouts under the dimming western stars. At least the sky had remained essentially the same, though for a time it had seemed that even it would be destroyed by the reek of the fuming earth. Far off she could see one of the Nevada smog towers, where gigantic fans sucked the pollutants from jets or mountain smelters down into the tower's whirring belly. Otherwise the landscape was empty, a lunar landscape of grays, browns, and skeleton whites.

"There's the sun!" Lester exclaimed softly and Zeb knew from the flash in his voice that he felt the same thrill she did. The sun was only a molten thread yet, but even the tiny portion that showed was enough to cast long, crooked shadows over the desolate vastness.

All along the highway, on each side, stretched the high, once-electrified fences, leftovers from the days when three fourths of the sprawling Western Reserve lands had been off limits to all but military personnel. Except for an isolated military post or radar station, the wilderness was empty. Peeling and faded warning signs remained at frequent intervals, proclaiming, DANGER: *Contaminated Zone. No Admittance.*

In the strengthening rays of the sun, the blighted soil resembled the sterile salt flats of Death Valley, testimony to the chemical-warfare experiments that had leaped out of control, along with herbicides and defoliants. Even before that, much of the land had been destroyed by nonmilitary means. Even far back in the California-gold-rush days, dredge mining had devoured acres, leaving only grassless boulders in its wake. No, despoliation of the environment was not new, Zebrina thought; only more sophisticated and deadly.

The fatal experiments were presumably over now, but no one knew when, if ever, the ravished earth, rivers, and air would completely recover. In spite of some earlier attempts by scientists, agronomists, and engineers to restore the land, nobody could tell when the fences around millions of acres could be safely removed. Perhaps never, simply because so few individuals cared any longer. They were far more interested, Zeb thought bitterly, in putting fences, machines, and cities on the moon or Mars. If, as she believed, much of the contamination had already been dissipated by nature's own recuperative powers, the mountains and forests still offered the recreation and beauty they had years before, except for the wildlife. If she were right, what then? Could some sharp-eyed developer reawaken the public interest in wilderness recreation, rebuilding the deserted ski lifts and lodges, promoting the idea of a "return to nature"? She shuddered at a vision of helicopters, hovercraft, and all the rest loaded with tourists, and concentrated on watching the ditches for one green blade of grass or the commonest weed.

The children had grown silent and she realized that the lifeless land had cast its spell over them. But there was no other route; even if there were, the same sad vistas would remain. They were headed south now, the abrupt slopes of the Sierra Nevada on their right, and she felt the sunlight begin to warm her left side.

Even though she had earlier asked for silence, it was now oppressive. "Did you know, my dears, that long ago this road was called El Camino Sierra? Of course, it was only an Indian trail at first, and then a wagon road. Whenever you begin to grow warm, children, I'll turn the air conditioner on." The night chill of the high desert regions could turn to heat with astonishing swiftness.

"If you keep an eye out," she chatted on, "you'll see evidences of ancient volcanic action. Streams and glaciers, as you already know, removed vast amounts of volcanic rock. It's truly a land sculptured by fire and ice. 'The burnt land,' as the Paiute Indians called it."

"And sculptured anew by DDT and nuclear explosions," Lester mumbled.

"It doesn't look much different from around New City," Sylvie said. She sat very upright, partly out of a subdued interest in the landscape, but mostly in order not to wrinkle the orange-and-brown camping outfit she had charged to her parents' account at New City's finest store. Orange was not her best color, she knew, but Aunt Zeb had insisted that their garb should be predominantly orange, as that was the easiest color to see in case somebody got lost. Not that anyone was going to, Zeb had said hastily.

Patrick pushed his visored orange cap up on his damp forehead, then removed it, and looked back at Sylvie. "How can the land be much different from the City when we've only gone fifty miles?" He consulted the map. "We've got almost two hundred miles before we reach the pass."

Sylvie smoothed a wrinkle in her hiking shorts. "As if I didn't know that!"

"I know it, too," Fay said, not wanting to be left out.

"Well," Lester said from his corner, "I think everything looks different already. For one thing, we scarcely ever escape the dome to see the sunrise. The last time was when we drove to Pyramid Lake for our overnight stay, last year."

"Some lake!" Patrick said sourly. He could see the withered shore line in his memory, and the thirty-mile-long hollow where once a sheet of water had glimmered. The water had been pumped out long ago for industrial purposes, leaving whatever Indians had been there without their source of fish or small game. Almost all that remained was the volcanic cone that had given the lake its name, and the strange tufa formation called "The Squaw with a Basket." The wind-eaten squaw, a large, faceless head balanced on a squat body, a crumbling, basket-shaped stone beside her, had struck Patrick as grotesque and forlorn. All around there was nothing but desert, but there had been no fences. The Pyramid area was on limits for sightseers, though only the hardiest campers went there. The Squad had had the place all to themselves except for an old Indian and his wife who clung to the spot and tried to barter some carved stone trinkets in exchange for money or food from the few travelers who appeared.

"We found artifacts there, nevertheless," Lester said. Under his cap's visor, tiny beads of perspiration clung to his dark, thick eyebrows.

Fay exclaimed, "I found the prize, remember? That obsidian pipe. Wasn't that the prize find, Aunt Zeb?"

"It was certainly very fine," Zeb answered. "But remember, it's cooperation, not competition, that counts. It will be especially essential on this journey. This time we are out for much bigger stakes."

Immediately the atmosphere of the car changed, the Squad recovering the excitement that had electrified them at the time of departure. Voices babbled again, with frequent references to "the animals," and even Knobs murmured something about a quest, without revealing exactly what it was. "I might find something, too, something different from anything."

Lester glanced back at her. "How different?"

Knobs shrugged under his exploring, intent gaze and pressed her nose again to the tail-gate window. He studied the bulge in the hip pocket of her shorts and recognized the shape of the jack boxes. The rubber ball made an additional bulge, straining the seams of the pocket. The jacks were a kind of obsession, he thought, a form of escape from reality. He had gone through a period like that once, after the night he had overheard his father and mother pitched against each other at such a peak of rage that they had threatened each other physically.

He had lain rigid in bed, fixed by anguish and horror, waiting for the sound of a shot or, at the least, an overturning of furniture. They had quieted at last, merely hissing at each other, but he had remained so unnerved that for many nights thereafter he woke regularly, expecting to hear the storming voices. It was around then that he had read about a toy, popular many years before, called a yo-yo. He had hunted down specific descriptions of the spool-like toy and had made one for himself. Attaching a long, supple cord to the spool, he had practiced hour after hour until he could make the yo-yo spin in almost any fashion he desired. Unlike Knobs, he had practiced in secret.

He still kept the yo-yo tucked in a cubicle of his room, but he seldom thought about it any more. It was an abandoned piece of his life, a childish artifact. Self-realization, he thought, lay not in toys and gadgets, but in the spirit. He tried now to withdraw inwardly from the babble of voices, scanning the monotony of the nearby landscape, the blue dream of the high-crested mountains rising abruptly and giddily from the desert land. The granite of their peaks was pale pink in the morning sun, and a mid-June snowfall shone dazzling white in their notches and crevices. The first thing he would do, he decided, when they reached there—if they reached there—would be to cup a handful of the whiteness to his face, tasting it and smelling its freshness. Snow, when it fell on New City dome, melted at once. Up there in the mountains, thousands of feet above sea level, was the only purity that remained. Trees, too. Perhaps drinkable streams. And animals! Honesty compelled him to put a big question mark after the last category.

There have to be animals, he thought. If not, the journey was a sham and a delusion. He studied the back of Aunt Zeb's head, the roughly clipped white hair edging out from under the rim of her helmet. Human beings were fallible, and she had not absolutely promised lions or fawns. Still, she had held out the glimmer. Once, it seemed like two years ago, or perhaps earlier, before his yo-yo period, she had been extremely agitated and flushed at one of the Squad meetings. It was either because of something she had seen and heard over the Electravision Service, or because of the intense heat that had existed in Old City for several days. Whatever it was, she had been abnormally wrought up with concern for the animals that had been extinct even before she was born.

Her husband, she said, had bragged that he had killed the last of the native American mountain lions. "But I don't believe him, dears!" she had declared. "It exists—they exist—out there in what remains of the wilderness. Indeed, I sometimes wonder about the great auk, and Steller's sea cow, and even the supposedly extinct sea mink. Can we be absolutely sure—of anything?"

No, Lester thought now, gazing out at the harsh glitter of rocks. If you looked hard enough, even at the dun land this side of the mountain range, there was a subtle beauty in the grays, whites, tans, and browns. Off to the west there was a brick-colored canyon cutting below the chemical salt-whiteness. Volcanic deposits had added masses of black, red, and pumice-gray. High above, in the jagged peaks of the Ritter Range, there was the radiance of glaciers.

Sweat trickled down the sides of his cheeks. Patrick, at Zeb's order, pulled the air-conditioning lever.

Lester wiped his forehead with his handkerchief. There was much to be said in favor of artificial environmental controls, for all that he loved the adventure of being outside the womblike covering of the dome. He derided himself for putting creature comfort foremost, and forced himself to recite twenty lines of Krishna as a penance.

The cool air was particularly welcome to Fay, crouched in her back corner. She was beginning to feel ill, partly because of Aunt Zeb's erratic style of driving. Zeb would zigzag absent-mindedly even on straight roads as she pointed out this or that object of interest. Now they had reached a stretch of low-mountain curves, the road looping back and forth on itself, a few dizzying drop-offs appearing at the highway's edge. Gazing down at them, swaying in the lurchings of the station wagon, Fay increasingly felt vertigo and an uneasiness at the pit of her stomach. The uneasiness turned to nausea. Her smile, when she tried to respond to some sally or quip of the three older members of the Squad, was wan.

Sylvie with her perceptive glance noticed, but instead of keeping it to herself she had to announce to everyone, "Fay looks absolutely green! She's getting carsick."

"I'm not either," Fay denied. "It's only the heat."

"You should have spoken up earlier, love," Aunt Zeb said over her shoulder. "Patrick, do you have the air conditioner on high?"

He leaned forward and adjusted the lever.

"I feel fine now," Fay said, but it was not true. On their last outing, she had been carsick almost to the point of vomiting. She had managed to avoid the final humiliation, but it still remained as a terror in her mind. The very thought of throwing up in front of all of them . . . She gripped her abdomen with one hand, her nerves tightening with apprehension. Then she saw Aunt Zeb's eyes in the rear-view mirror, studying her.

There was a spot of shade in the road ahead where a bulbous outcropping of rock stood up around a small, twisting ravine. The fences around the contaminated zone were several hundred feet back from the road.

Zeb slowed the car. "It's time we all took a break, I think." She steered toward a pull-out spot in the shade. "We have to make our own rest stops, after all, and not depend on nonexistent comfort stations. Anyhow, I could do with a stretch of my legs."

Fay felt a rush of gratitude, though Zeb stopped the car none too soon. Pushing Knobs ahead of her, Fay rushed through the automatically opened tail gate and hurried toward a comparatively private spot behind the gnarled rocks. Her cheeks were puffed out and she was forced to clap one hand over her mouth, even at the risk of the others' seeing, before she reached her refuge. There she spewed up most of her share of the breakfast Aunt Zeb had provided everyone, choking and heaving, her eyes running tears.

The only person who saw was Knobs, who came bumbling around the rocks, scrawny fingers working at the side
zipper of her shorts. She squatted down, murmuring, "I'm
glad you got sick, Fay, or maybe Auntie Zeb wouldn't have
stopped. I had to go something awful."

Fay straightened, looking away from the little trickle
where Knobs squatted.

"You won't tell them, will you, Knobs? About my being
sick, I mean."

There was the closest thing to a smile on Knobs's squinty
little face that Fay had ever seen. "I didn't see nothin',"
she replied.

They regarded each other, and Fay felt a sweet sense of
relief and sudden comradeship. It had been nice, staying at
Sylvie's apartment the night before, but it had been
strained too, because Fay had felt intimidated by the
luxury of her surroundings. Sylvie had tried to make her
feel relaxed, but the strain had remained.

Fay made a movement, thinking to link Knobs's arm in
hers, but Knobs drew back and she knew she was over-
reaching. "Come on, Knobby," she said, "before we get
sunstroke. These brimmed caps Aunt Zeb made us wear
aren't much help." She wondered what it would be like to
lose the protection of the car, if they did. Probably it
wouldn't happen very soon.

As she and Knobs returned to the station wagon, they
saw Aunt Zeb and the others returning from their individual sorties.

" 'Give me the splendid silent sun,' " Aunt Zeb quoted
from Walt Whitman, " 'with all his beams full-dazzling.' "
She looked around her, head thrust back, full-breasted

chest pushed out, a figure of exultation, eyes shining through the thick glasses. "Let us share a toast, treasures, with some cool, blessed water from the canteens."

They looked at the vast wasteland, the blue sheen of the neighboring mountains, and solemnly raised their canteens. The rocky crests sparkled in the rising light, far beyond fences and beyond the end of El Camino Sierra.

"A toast," Aunt Zeb repeated. "Come, we need a poet." She looked toward Patrick, though it was Lester she had in mind.

Patrick, sturdy though he was, dedicated and strong, looked suddenly shy. "Well—uh—to the journey," he said lamely. But he waited, not raising his canteen.

Lester drew in a deep breath. *"Blessed of the Lord be his land,"* he intoned self-consciously, stumbling over the words, *"for the precious things of heaven, for the dew . . . ."* He paused, struggled to remember. "And, uh— *and for the chief things of the ancient mountains, and for the precious things of the lasting hills."* He shrugged self-deprecatingly, then lifted the canteen slowly to his mouth.

They piled back into the station wagon, Aunt Zeb still claiming the wheel.

Deuteronomy. Zebrina reflected on Lester's quotation. She had been certain it would be the *Gita* or something even more exotic. Well, it had been appropriate enough. Lester's literary sources, bless him, were many. As for dear, steady Patrick . . . She glanced at him, his firm hand clutching the maps, the twisty cowlicks in his hair rebelling against his early-morning attempts at brushing them into submission.

*Well—uh—to the journey.*

She smiled, her heart warm, loving both Lester and Patrick. All of them. Did the setter and the dear little grizzled Boston bull, and Goldie, and the banty hens miss her yet? she wondered. Probably not too much, she admitted, even though it hurt to think that doting humans were not all that important in self-doting animal lives. Anyhow, Steve would care for them conscientiously.

The mountains were closer. She pressed down on the accelerator, drawing the peaks and whatever they concealed toward her. There was a throb of excitement in her fingers gripping the wheel. She pressed back doubt and trepidation.

"To the journey!" she said, and the other members of the Squad echoed the phrase in lusty unison.

# CHAPTER 6

THE sky was empty except for the steady progression of cargo and transport planes off toward the Pacific coast and several thunderheads building up over the mountains. Watching the planes from behind the steering wheel, Zebrina reflected that what she missed most was the sight of turkey vultures wheeling their black shoulders against the sky. Songless though the vultures were, unless their rasping *burr* of a cry could be called a song, they had been an integral part of the landscape. And their scavenging beaks had helped to keep the earth clean.

The sun was overhead before Zeb began searching for a suitable place for lunch. The road had deteriorated steadily as they gained altitude; it was heaved by frost boils, pitted by errant floodwaters. Along the way, the ruins of cabins, cafés, and gasoline stations gave an extra touch of melancholy to the land. At the height of the Contamination, as it was called, owners and tourists had fled. Now the populace was imprisoned by psychological conditioning. Just as the slopes of Old City were considered dangerous, so the wilderness remained a threat. It was a reversal of the pioneering spirit of frontier times, when the very word "wilderness" had symbolized freedom and opportunity. The people in the domed cities—and all the large cities were enclosed under Plexiglas (like dead partridges sealed in glass tombs, Zeb thought)—clung to their security. Astrodome sports, which included everything from track meets to golf, had replaced the onetime summer exodus of city people to the country.

"I'm starvin'," Knobs said for the third time in the past hour.

"I know, love. We all are. But we wouldn't much enjoy eating our lunch in the boiling sun." Zebrina searched the road ahead, vaguely remembering from years past that there was a pull-out to a rest area in this vicinity. Even in the days of steady tourist traffic there had been a scarcity of such welcome rest stops.

"It's boiling here in the car, too," Patrick said. "The air conditioner can't cope." He looked at the air-temperature gauge. "Eighty-one, Aunt Zeb."

"It will moderate once we get higher, but a scrap of shade in this chaparral would be welcome."

Just when she had nearly given up hope, the *Rest Area* sign appeared around a bend. Like the warning signs on the government fences, it was faded almost beyond legibility. Most of the trees once planted around the place had withered under the poisons accidentally sprayed over them, one of the frequent mishaps that had occurred at the height of the chemical experimentations. But a single stubborn piñon remained, and the roofboards of the open-sided shelter itself were still in place.

"How marvelously enduring wood can be!" Aunt Zeb exclaimed, steering toward the parking area.

"Maybe we'd be better off if people were made of wood," Lester said.

The remark was ignored in the general relief at finding some shade where the lunch hamper could be opened and its contents enjoyed. There was only enough of what Zeb called "live" food to provide for this lunch and perhaps one or two more meals. After that they would have to depend on concentrated and dehydrated foods. No more sliced ham or egg salad or lettuce, but only the kind of food that could be carried on their backs in knapsacks. Dried milk, for instance, instead of the fresh milk from the Dairy Dome now riding in the portable refrigerator.

Stepping out of the car, Patrick felt the blast of the desert heat. For an instant he half enjoyed it, the sense of being pitted against its invisible but potent force. He looked about him, nearly blinded in spite of his dark glasses by the naked glitter of the surrounding sand, rocks, and salt-encrusted wastes. Again, as in the attic, he had a vision of himself trudging doggedly across such a landscape, lugging a comrade over his shoulders. Rescuer. Hero. Then he felt the heat striking down to the roots of his hair, tunneling even into his ears. He yearned toward the shade though he dutifully turned back to help Aunt Zeb, Lester, and the others lug the lunch containers toward the wreck of a table under the weather-battered roof. Belatedly, he took his cap from the car seat and put it on.

" 'Fools' names and fools' faces,' " Fay recited, " 'always appear in public places.' " Both table and roof supports were covered with jackknife hieroglyphics. *Jim loves Anne. Tom Rounds, 1985.* A crudely carved heart enclosed the names, *Phoebe and Ron.* Even the lone piñon bore the scars of initials and designs carved years before.

Most impressive, Patrick thought, was the silence. In New City there was always a hum, in spite of the almost noiseless electric cars and buses, the rubber moving sidewalks, the acoustical absorbency of building and dome. He could almost feel his heat-seared ears stretching to try to catch some murmur or whisper from the vastness. The chatter of voices as Aunt Zeb placed the food on the table and began serving only accentuated the stillness of the background. Looking beyond the silent flats to the equally silent mountains, Patrick felt goose-pimples rise on his forearms. To have goose-pimples in such heat was ridiculous, and he hoped that no one had noticed. They might think the sudden tiny bumps were the product of fear.

I'm not afraid, he told himself. He glanced back over his shoulder toward the car, thinking of the rifle lying there, the protective meters and gauges, the first-aid kit, the emergency rations, and knew that he was lying to himself.

He regarded the others. They all seemed relaxed, gobbling their food while he still held his untasted ham sandwich in one hand. Doubt shook him. His vision of Patrick Day, hero, lugging a stricken Fay or Knobs or even Aunt Zeb on his back across stretches of burning sand, changed miserably to a picture of himself as the rescued weakling.

It was absurd. It was the result of the heat and the impact of the unimaginable silence. He had never lacked courage or endurance as far as he could remember. Quite the opposite. He had prided himself, always, on his fortitude. Perhaps the long, lonely endurance runs had not been a real test. Yet they had hardened him—his muscles were surely far firmer than Lester's.

He nibbled at his sandwich and watched Lester from the corner of his eye. Lester stood apart, leaning against one of the shelter supports, chewing on his own sandwich, drinking the cold milk, in a dreamy, languid manner. His gaze was fixed on the far distances, as Patrick's had been, but he looked inspired rather than intimidated. Patrick half expected him to sit down suddenly and cross his legs in an attitude of meditation. Instead, Lester looked across at Patrick, smiled crookedly, one cheek bulging with food, and said, "It's tremendous—you can see eternity in every corner. I mean, the air's so clear." He let his breath out softly. "This is going to be—I don't know. A real trip, right over the edge."

"I hope you brought a parachute, then," Patrick responded lightly, trying to escape both Lester's overreaction, as it seemed to him, and his own treacherous self-doubt. "Anyhow, it will be an adventure."

"Here, look," Aunt Zeb was saying, bending over so far that her nose was only a couple of feet from the ground. "See how a manzanita grove struggled for survival. Look, dears, at those gnarled and valiant roots." She stooped even more, then got down on her knees, staring. "There's a green shoot here! Green life!" She pressed her hand to her heart like an actress in an old-fashioned melodrama. "But, oh, it's so dry . . ." She glanced somewhat wildly toward the sky, one hand cupped as if to receive rain. "It will never survive without help. Sylvie—Knobs—somebody bring a canteen. We can share our portion, surely, with this little green, struggling thing."

Knobs, surprisingly, was the swiftest volunteer, loping to the car and returning at a knock-kneed run with her own canteen. "It can have my portion," she said.

"Bless you, sweet," Zeb said, taking the canteen, unscrewing the plastic cap, and then slowly, tenderly, pouring the precious water over the young shoot. "If we could save this one green thing, it would be worth the trip. Don't you agree, Squad? Our chance arrival here could make all the difference between life and death. On our way back we'll attend to it again."

"If there's any water left by then," Patrick said.

Aunt Zeb's gaze swiveled slowly toward him. "But, of course, we'll have water, darling. There's the reserve tank in the car, as you well know. And we should have enough for our own uses up there." She indicated the mountains. "There's the melting, unsullied snow, and fresh springs, surely."

He felt her eyes appraising him and saw the surprise in them. He shrugged, trying to pass off his unjustified doubt. He and Zeb had carefully studied the water problem, and up until this moment he had been completely optimistic. The heat dug and clawed at his scalp again in spite of the cap and the shade of the warped roof. "I only mentioned, wondered . . ." he mumbled, feeling terribly lightheaded. "Maybe I'd better sit down."

The desert world went black and Patrick Day, hero and rescuer, fainted before the Squad's astonished eyes. The next thing he knew, cool canteen water was splashing over his face, running into his eyes and the corners of his mouth.

He shook himself and struggled up on one elbow. "No—

save it for the roots!" he exclaimed, still only half-conscious.

Aunt Zeb had one arm under him. "Rest a bit, sweet, and you'll be all right. Some people are much more susceptible to sunlight than others. And, remember, you've been living under the dome for a long while. It takes time to become acclimated."

He sat up groggily, with Zeb's assistance, and saw Sylvie looking down at him with an expression that combined sympathy and doubt.

He hated sympathy, especially from Sylvie. "I'm O.K.!" he declared, wavering to his feet. He tried to conceal his shakiness, pushed his hands into the pockets of his shorts to steady himself, and clenched his teeth. "D'you want me to take over the wheel from here on, Aunt Zeb?" he asked. "Time you had a rest."

She studied him, hearing both the demand and the appeal in his voice. "That was what I was going to suggest, dear—if you feel all right."

"Feel fine," Patrick said and strode toward the car. He clamped his hands around the steering wheel, confidence returning. He should have driven from the start, he thought. It was hard for him to be a passenger, dependent on the skills of others. But to drive, to lead, to take responsibility . . .

Yet he was haunted by the memory of his momentary weakness. It was one thing for Fay to become carsick, but for him to pass out, right there in front of everybody, was complete humiliation. He looked at the rough road snaking higher and higher ahead.

"You're sure you feel up to it?" Aunt Zeb asked as she slid onto the passenger's side of the seat.

Patrick nodded. "Sure." When the rest were inside the car, he put the transmission into drive. "That was only a freak thing," he assured Zeb, though the assertion was meant for the others as well.

"Maybe there were fumes left over from the chemicals— or nerve gas," Sylvie said.

There was a tense, apprehensive silence.

Zebrina waved her hand in front of her face. "Nonsense, dear. Let's not imagine things worse than they are. My meter reading here showed only minimal contamination, as I foresaw. I wouldn't have brought you here otherwise. The sun was too much for our Patrick, that's all. Now, let's relax and watch for whatever is green, growing, creeping, flying. We have a quest, remember."

Carefully, though nervously, Patrick steered the wagon up the gradually ascending road. With each passing minute his confidence was restored. The sunstroke, or whatever, had been only a fluke. The Squad would find out that there was no reason to doubt his sturdiness.

If there's a question of survival, he thought as he drove on, I will survive. I have to, because I am Patrick. But who was Patrick? Me, he answered, and recalled one night when his father had staggered against all the furniture in the apartment, appealing, "Hey, Pat, give a hand."

He had crawled out of bed, feet bare, and striven to support his father's one-hundred-and-eighty-pound weight with his own. Except for its grimness, it could have been a clown act on TV. Tears had streamed down Dad's face as

Dad had cried with guilt and remorse. "I've been a lousy father and husband, Pat. But everything was always against me. You'll find out when you get to be a man. And you'll be a man someday. Don't make the mistakes I made. I'm counting on you. You're going to have to make up for everything I wasn't, Pat. Just remember that."

Patrick hit a rut and the car bounced. He could feel the tension all around him.

"I'm glad you're driving," Aunt Zeb said. "The road is fierce. We may not be able to go as far on it as we hoped." She turned toward the back seat. "Let's play the 'animal, vegetable, or mineral' game for a while."

They did, with enjoyment. In the midst of it all, Knobs somehow cleared a space on the jolting floor of the rear deck and attempted to play with her jacks.

*Tap-thud-clack.* The precise, tapping sound blended with the hum of the motor. It was a somewhat reassuring sound, and Patrick felt his hands relax on the steering wheel.

They continued on, up and up, toward the pass, toward where the animals were or once had been, and might, miraculously, still be.

# CHAPTER 7

THEY were at moderately high altitude, but still in arid country on the steep eastern side of the Sierra Nevada, when they reached what seemed a likely camp spot for the night. Though most of the brush and small trees on the site had perished, the spot was level and had a stream trickling along one side. Whether the water was pure or not no one could know until Zebrina tested it, but the sight of it splashing and gleaming in the pre-sunset glow was refreshing. Anyhow, there was not much choice. The road was becoming all but nonexistent. Further, everyone was showing signs of fatigue.

"What do you think, Squad?" Zeb said from the front seat. She had made up her mind that they ought to stop here but she did not want to be a dictator. "It will be dark soon and this seems a reasonable spot. To tell the truth, I'm tuckered out." So was Patrick, she thought, seeing the shadows under his large, thickly lashed eyes. He would never admit it, of course, and under ordinary circumstances she would not have let him drive for so many hours at one stretch. But she knew he was trying to prove his strength, and she did not want to interfere.

"It looks all right to me," Sylvie said. Her crisp orange-and-brown costume had lost its freshness, and she no longer cared.

Knobs, half-asleep in the rear, mumbled, "I'm tired of ridin'." She saw the stream. "Oh, lookit—it's real live water. We could go wadin'!"

Lester closed the book he had been reading: *Revolutionary Ideas of Mankind*. "There's firewood. It would help us save fuel, for cooking."

Fay said, "What do you think, Aunt Zeb?"

"I think this is it," Zeb answered. "Watch out for the rocks, Patrick—pull off to the right there so we can have a level spot for the tent trailer. Good, dear. That's fine."

Patrick maneuvered, brought the car to a halt, and unclamped his fingers from the steering wheel. It was a relief to step out of the vehicle and stand upright, breathing the open air again. There was a cool desert breeze blowing, and the silver light of a young moon was a refreshing contrast to the bloody crimson of the sinking sun.

Aunt Zeb calibrated her test meters, took the essential readings, and then, assuming the stance of a military major, said crisply, "Everybody to his station. There's much to be done."

There was, and she observed with pride how well the Squad went about their duties. True, they had rehearsed their roles back home, but rehearsal and the actual thing were often different. With a minimum of fumbling, Lester and Patrick pitched the umbrella tent, while Aunt Zeb and the girls raised and secured their own canvas shelter on its trailer base. Within a half hour the two tents were in place, and Zebrina gave a sigh of content. She had always loved tents, those portable houses that changed any wilderness into a tidy homestead. Though she hated the hunting part of the trips with James, making camp had enchanted her. As it did now, even among the ruins of what had been.

"Can I go wadin'?" Knobs asked.

"Yes, love," Zeb had made a cursory check on the water, among her many other activities. "There's no danger as long as you avoid drinking it until I've had a chance to give it a more thorough inspection. But first things first. Blow up your air mattresses, arrange nearby all the things you need or may need—flash, matches, canteen. Well, you know the routine." She looked back toward the dusty car, lists spinning in her mind. Food was the first essential; and as Lester had said, for their fuel, they would be wise to use the dead wood lying around like the bleached bones of animals.

"Once you've all got your sleeping spots shipshape," she advised, "go ahead and do whatever you wish. I'll prepare the fire and the supper. But when I blow the whistle"—she indicated the metal whistle on the cord around her neck—"I expect you to convene here at once. You remember the other rules—never drink untested water, always watch for signs of new vegetation, animal tracks, or living creatures." She did not mention wild-dog bands. There had been no sign of such and the chances were that they would not venture this far from human habitations, if any still survived.

The group listened politely, obviously bored, eager to explore the site for whatever surprises it might hold.

All but Fay turned away, scattering toward the creek. "I'll help you get dinner, Aunt Zeb," she offered.

In spite of her chunky body, she looked small and even frail against the immensity of the sunset.

"Don't you want to go and explore with the others, treasure?"

Fay nibbled at a finger nail. "I really want to work on this trip. I mean, I plan on lots of hiking and exercise. If you sweat a lot, you can lose maybe five pounds a day."

"Why, sweetheart," Zeb said, "you can sweat and work all you wish. But I don't want to have a skinny Fay. What would I put my arms around then?" She gave the girl a hug, then led the way toward piles of desert driftwood close by. "We'll start the fire, and then I think I'll splash my poor old feet in the sparkling stream myself."

Feeling self-important and satisfied, Fay began hauling wood toward a cook spot Aunt Zeb had hastily marked out with a stroke of her heavy-soled hiking shoes.

"Wouldn't it be wonderful if we really did find something alive?" Fay said as she delivered an armload of the dry, crackling brush on the site. "Like a little fox, I mean. Foxes don't bite, do they?"

"Everything bites, child, when frightened. Not out of viciousness. But when any creature thinks it's in danger, it naturally tries to protect itself."

"They wouldn't be in danger from me. I wouldn't ever hurt anything."

"I know you wouldn't, Fay dear." Zeb made a small wigwam of sticks, breaking them to the right size in her hands, and giving thicker branches an expert chop with the short ax. "If you want to find some larger pieces now . . ." she coached while she dragged a number of boulders into a circle around the tinder. From a waterproof container she removed a match, struck it, and held it to the dead, dried grass mixed in with the twigs.

Behind her she could hear the splash of water as the young people waded or tossed rocks into the stream.

"It's as cold as ice!" Sylvie complained loudly.

"Water can never be colder than thirty-two degrees," Patrick said authoritatively.

"Why not?"

"Because then it would freeze and be ice, not water, obviously."

Patrick was right, of course, Zeb thought as she gave the fresh flames a helpful puff and then stood back to watch, contentedly, the zealous blaze. Only she wished Pat would be a bit more considerate of Sylvie's ego. Oh, well, it was only natural for youngsters to scrap and compete for first place. And, in any case, it was a delight to hear their splashings and unrestrained voices, especially that of Knobs.

"My feet are freezin'!" Knobs cried, but there was pleasure in the cry. Zeb thought: Whatever comes of the trip it will be especially good for Knobs—Celeste. Good for all of them. Perhaps, most of all, good for herself. She had been depressed of late, even morbid at times, too much caught up in her own thoughts and her fears about the future development of the world. She looked toward the new moon, thinking of the structures being built there, and the most recent space station rotating in the void. No doubt, man was driven to seek homes beyond the earth for the reason that the earth had been nearly destroyed. Well, she would not live to see the colonies on Mars or Jupiter. But the youngsters would. She sighed and saw Fay studying her own shadow, stretched out long and lavender in the sun's last rays.

"Shadows are funny, aren't they?" Fay said. "It looks like I'm a long, skinny giant stretched out on the ground. Do you need any more wood, Aunt Zeb?" She was perspiring from her exertions and glanced longingly toward the stream.

"No. We'll have the boys haul in some larger pieces for our evening fire. This is fine, and while I let it settle down to coals, let's join the water babies."

Fay flashed her a questioning look.

"*The Water Babies* was a book I read, and adored, a thousand years ago, child. Let's see now—oh, yes." She fumbled through her luggage and removed a plastic case containing the chief water-testing device. Included in the kit were chlorine and other tablets to purify polluted water in small quantities for drinking.

When she reached the edge of the stream, followed by Fay, she removed her boots and socks, then stepped gingerly into the shallow water, giving a shriek that more than satisfied her grinning audience.

"Sylvie's absolutely right," she said with a shiver. "It is ice, perhaps even a bit colder. Where's Lester?"

"He went off to meditate somewhere," Sylvie answered.

"He'd better not meditate too long," Aunt Zeb said, surveying the darkening land. He couldn't possibly get lost in such a comparatively open area, she told herself, and applied herself to the water test. The device was intricate but compact and simple to operate. Injecting a sample of water into the fill tube, she pressed a button that activated the power source. The gadget hummed and ticked and the needle on the numbered dial face moved slowly from its zero position. The numerals on the dial went to one hundred. Any water sample that registered sixty or over was safe for consumption.

Zebrina and the others watched the indicator. "Forty," Sylvie counted aloud. "Forty-five. Fifty!"

The needle wavered, moved forward again a fraction, and then stopped at fifty-four.

Zeb sighed and shut off the mechanism. "It was too much to hope for, Squad, at this altitude."

"It'll be different when we get high up, won't it?" Fay asked.

"Oh, yes, dear. Of course. Well, I must go back to my fire, to dry my feet, if nothing else." She glanced around the rocky, canyon-creased landscape once more, wondering about Lester. Perhaps he had only needed to use the "facilities." Or, if he truly were meditating, she hated to disturb him before necessary. Not bothering to lace her boots, she strode back toward the fire, tripping once over the laces. One by one, the others followed to gather close to the flames, chilled by the water and by the cooling air.

In a matter of minutes, everyone helping—for Zebrina carefully included a task for each—fresh lamb chops in special wire holders were broiling slowly over the red coals, potatoes started to simmer in a separate niche, and on another corner of the rude rock stove, fresh asparagus waited its turn.

"We're living off the fat of the land—the fat of the Agri-labs, I mean," Zeb said. "Tonight. Tomorrow night we may be on our own, down to fundamentals, unless the road suddenly improves. If not, it will be backpacking."

"That will be good exercise," Fay said.

Sylvie was looking dreamily off at the last pale shreds of the sunset. "I wish I could paint well. I'd make a painting of that sky for my mother and father. But I'm not good enough."

"You are too, darling," Aunt Zeb insisted. "Simply print the whole scene on your mind and when you are back home you'll be able to create a beautiful picture." She sat down on a folding stool Patrick had brought for her from the car, testing the potatoes with a long fork. "I do wish Lester would show up. He's been gone quite long enough."

"I'll go look for him," Patrick volunteered. He was feeling fine now. It seemed as if the silly fainting spell earlier had happened to somebody else.

"You'll do no such thing, love," Zeb declared. "It's too dark to go stumbling around in unknown terrain. He'll be along presently. But just to hurry him up, there's this." She lifted her whistle and gave it a shrill blast.

The whistle was clear enough to Lester's ears, although he was surprised at its remoteness. He had wandered farther than he realized. First, he had separated from the group only because he craved relief from the noisy conversations in the car followed by the general boisterousness of the wading scene. He wanted to experience the deep silence of the area, and hear the creaking rocks. For it seemed, in such a plain of silence, that they must have some sound, no matter how faint. Rocks were never dead things to him, any more than the Squaw with a Basket at Pyramid Lake was. He saw all rocks, whether boulders or pebbles or mountains, as interlaced with veins and gristle, frozen arteries and rigid lace. Animals and vegetation had been swallowed up in them. Who knew what strange bones, and even brains, were a part of volcanic flows? At certain exalted moments he was convinced that he had heard rocks grunt in bitter heat, and pebbles gasp. He could not prove it, however, and he had never expressed such beliefs to anyone, not even to Aunt Zeb, who would have understood and very likely agreed.

Certainly, the rocks here were silent. That was all right, since he was in the mood for silence. There was only the crunch of his boot soles against sand and gravel, and the scratchy whisper of wind stirring the soil or rattling the remains of a dead bush or tree. He had roamed for a half an hour or so when he thought he saw, or dreamed he saw, tiny animal tracks. It was difficult to know, in the swiftly fading light, and he had not brought his flash.

His throat dry with excitement, Lester knelt and studied the tracks—if that was what they were. The patterns in the sand were delicate and scrambled, almost as if a tumbleweed had rolled erratically across the ground. Yet in the midst of the intricate path there did seem to be the marks of small foot pads or claws. The vague and confusing trail wavered uncertainly between two clumps of reddish-gray rocks, disappeared, and then reappeared about one hundred feet beyond. Rediscovering them, Lester wanted to call to the others. He was already too far, then, to make them hear—or, if he could, he decided he might only alarm them. Anyhow, if the tracks had been made by a tumbleweed or some other uprooted, dead plant, he would look like an idiot.

He followed the indistinct trail for another ten or fifteen feet and then there was nothing but the sand, rocks, and rubble. A decayed truck tire lay off to one side of a rock cleft and he looked at it with wonder. How it had got there, so far from the highway, was a mystery. The beer and pop cans that littered the landscape were explainable enough. Years ago, campers and hikers had brought their metal treasures with them, and left them. Eggshells, too, even in this remote spot.

Eggshells, he thought, even though broken to fragments, were as immortal as plastic. Finding a level slope of rock, he sat down to rest before his return to camp. The setting sun, on the opposite side of the earth from where it had been this morning, was a red-gold thread again. Above it, like a curved silver blade, was the moon. He gazed at the scene, head back, his hands clamped around his knees. Even if the Squad reached no farther than this, it was worth it, he thought. He breathed deeply, and then deliberately held his breath, listening to the silence.

He should have brought his Foreverflash, he realized, looking back across the graying land. Still, there would be no problem. No woods obscured the way, and the scrap of moon would be a help. He touched the bush knife at his belt, the canteen, and the compass secured in his hip-pocket case. He removed the compass, opened its lid, and slid the lever to free the needle, idly curious as to direction. He had guessed that in his rock seat he was facing south by southwest. He laid the compass on a horizontal patch of rock, and the wavering needle settled into place, pointing north. According to the compass he *was* facing south by southwest. He felt pleased with his sense of direction.

There was a faint sound, like a scrabble of claws. Lester restrained himself from leaping up. He waited, and thought he heard the sound again. Cautiously, slowly, he moved from the rock shelf, peering through the gloom. The few crooked shadows that remained in the last glance of the sun took on all sorts of fantastic shapes so that he imagined that there, alongside one boulder, was a fox—and there, in a crescent of tumbled granite, a porcupine. He edged forward, striving to separate reality from fantasy. He found nothing.

It had all been a product of his overeager imagination, he decided, looking glumly around him. He would not mention any of it back at camp. He turned to leave at the same moment that he heard a singing whine near his cheek. He straightened, startled. There was a stinging sensation. Involuntarily he slapped his cheek. When he drew his hand away, he saw the long-legged insect there, its wings and stinger crumpled.

He had studied his biology books enough to know what it was, though it was the first time in his life that he had ever suffered a mosquito bite.

"Wow!" he exclaimed in a most unmystic fashion. He started racing toward the camp even as he heard the remote whistle. With a sprinter's swift stride, he covered the distance speedily, dodging rocks and shadows, his chest bursting with the good news he had to tell.

He came gasping into camp and saw Aunt Zeb turn toward him, the firelight freckling her relieved features.

"I found something!" Lester yelled. "A mosquito! Here.

I brought it back. I know that's what it is!" He held his hand out, palm up, to Zebrina. "Isn't it?" Lester appealed. "It stung me. See?" He fingered the welt on his cheek.

"Ah," Zeb said softly, peering at the creature through her glasses. "Yes, Lester! It is. Indeed, it is! To think that I would ever feel joy over such—if only you knew what torments I have suffered from these tiny bombers. Oh, how lovely—how wonderful! Food for frogs and bats. And if there is food for them, there will be food for other creatures. Lester, love, I knight thee!" She drew him toward her and kissed his forehead. "For this, you deserve the biggest chop." She looked questioningly at the others.

They cheered and nodded.

"Run and put the specimen in our collection box, dear," Aunt Zeb instructed Lester. "Then we will feast."

It was a triumphant, happy group that sat under the fresh moon and the brightening stars, the smoke smell of the fire around them, combined with the sweet, crusty taste of the chops and the green-earth taste of potatoes and asparagus.

"I like it out here," Knobs said. "There ain't any freeways, neither."

"That is certainly the truth, treasure," Aunt Zeb said with a laugh, thinking about the troublesome road and the prospects for tomorrow.

Dishes done, all things prepared for morning, they settled into their quarters. Air mattresses were soft against the hardness of earth or trailer cot. Sleeping bags were cloth wombs against the night chill.

Far off, glinting in the starlight, lay the Squad's one compass.

# CHAPTER 8

LESTER stirred restlessly in his sleeping bag, envying Patrick, who was already snoring. He was overstimulated, Lester decided, by the discovery of the mosquito and Zeb's excitement thereafter, and by his own private experience of the sunset when he had been out among the rocks. Still, underneath the surface emotions, he felt a nagging uneasiness that he could not identify.

He turned over once more, determined to sleep, reciting a litany from his Yoga textbook. It was no help that he had pumped too much air into his air mattress, so that it was almost unyielding. He fumbled in the darkness for the flat, round release valve. The slight hiss of escaping air would not disturb so sound a sleeper as Patrick. His fingers found the valve, and instantly he forgot sleep or comfort. The round shape of the valve, its diameter almost that of a pocket compass, brought him up on his elbow in horrified realization. The compass! He had left it lying out there on a slab of rock! His heart beat so hard he feared Patrick could hear it as he stared through the gap in the tent fly toward the star-studded landscape beyond. Could he find his way back to it? He had to. The compass had been his responsibility.

Slowly, carefully, he unzipped the side of the bag, then eased his legs out on to the canvas floor. Patrick stopped snoring and Lester froze, stopping a hand in mid-air as he groped for his shoes. Patrick mumbled something unintelligible, then resumed his tranquil snores.

Trying to keep his own breathing shallow and every movement noiseless, Lester hauled his trousers over his briefs, pulled his desert boots on over bare feet, and found his sweater among the clothes folded at the foot of his bed. Seizing his flash, he moved toward the door and with unsteady fingers managed to undo the fly fastenings. Once safely out, he let the cloth flap drape back over the opening so that Patrick would not be wakened by the starlight. One of the differences between them was that Patrick liked his sleeping quarters as dark as possible, whereas Lester loved seeing some portion of sky. So they had compromised, covering the door but leaving the curtain up on one side window. The moon had shone through the window earlier, but now it had set.

Though he was safely outside the tent, Lester still did not dare to move without caution. He looked across at the other tent. There was no light there or any sound. Aunt Zeb and the girls had quieted well before he and Patrick had settled down, so the chances were very good that they were sound asleep.

Nevertheless, Lester crossed the campsite almost on tiptoe. Not until he had reached the other side of the road did he permit himself to quicken his pace. Then, with large rocks screening him from view of the tents, he took the Foreverflash from his belt and aimed its beam at the ground, hoping that he might find his own tracks. He had a general memory of the path he had followed earlier and recalled definitely that when he had sat on the rock slab, the compass beside him, he had been facing south by southwest. He looked up, studying the constellations. The Big Dipper was brilliantly clear, its outer edge pointing toward the glowing North Star. Using that as his sky compass, Lester trotted as rapidly as he dared across the rock-strewn land, fearful of stumbling.

All he needed, he thought, was a broken leg or a sprained ankle! That would mean the end of the trip for everybody.

He paused after what he judged was twenty minutes, searching around him for some landmark he might recognize. Even though the light had not been much stronger at dusk when he had made his way back to camp, the landscape now had a different tone under full starlight. It was more ghostly, even the largest boulders seeming to be spun out of gossamer. He slipped and struck one shin painfully against an outcropping and thought ruefully that the rocks were anything but fluff.

He went on, peering ahead, certain that he was nearing the spot where he had rested at sunset. There was a sound. Not near, and yet close enough to bring a feeling of ice into his veins. It was an unmistakable, shrill bark. Lester stood motionless, his scalp seeming to shrink. He waited a full minute. There was no further sound. Had he dreamed it?

It doesn't have to be a wild dog, he told himself. It could have been a fox—if there were any foxes still alive. Or maybe a wolf. But that was fantasy. Wolves, except possibly in remote regions of Alaska or Canada, had been extinct for decades. Anyhow, would it be any better to meet a wolf than a wild dog? Wolves, he had read, were shy animals, quick to flee at a human's approach. Wild dogs were another thing, especially if they were in a pack.

Whatever creature had given the bark, there was no sign of it anywhere in the immediate vicinity. Even so, Lester wished that he had some weapon with him as he moved forward warily. About one hundred feet ahead was a square, flat block of stone that looked familiar. It was obscured by several large boulders just this side of it, but he was certain it was the one where he had left the compass.

He hurried on with a sharp sense of relief. He would recover the compass, make his way back, and with any luck on his return, nobody would ever know. He stopped, thinking that he had heard the crackle of a dry twig breaking under a moving weight. Looking down, he saw twigs under his own feet. Quickly he rounded the boulders in his way and then froze.

The compass lay in plain sight, its metallic sides reflecting the starlight. But it was no longer on the rock. It lay, instead, about three feet away in a bed of dully shining pebbles. Only five feet beyond it stood the dog.

It was unquestionably a dog, though a grotesque mongrel unlike any dog Lester had ever seen. It resembled more the hyenas he had seen in the New City zoo with its large head, small eyes, and thin hindquarters. In spite of his terror, Lester felt a flash of pity, for the ragged animal was all but a skeleton. Even in the dim light, he could see the sharp circles of its ribs, the sunken hollows of its belly, the stringy haunches. Was there more than one dog? That was the question that throbbed in his mind as he recalled a story he had read about what had happened to certain lonely travelers when confronted by a wild pack. Normally the packs roamed closer to the cities, or military bases, for they were almost totally dependent on whatever food they could glean from the accidental droppings of garbage trains that carried city refuse to huge underground dump stations or to recycling plants.

Whatever the reason, this dog was here and, apparently, alone. The lone survivor, perhaps, of what had been a band.

Neither Lester nor the dog moved. Between them the compass gleamed, and Lester yearned to reclaim it. He held back, confronted by the menace of the mottled, watching shape, head hanging low, dark ears pricking the luminous, stark landscape. The dog neither barked at him nor growled. It stood silent, waiting for Lester to make the first move.

If I shine the flash directly into his eyes, Lester thought frantically, maybe I can blind him while I rush in and grab the compass. He aimed the light experimentally toward the animal and saw the dog's eyes glow as they caught the brilliance. The dog shied around briefly, then took up its watching stance again.

Lester picked up a stone the size of a baseball. His voice breaking, he cried, "Get out of here!" He waved his left arm while he kept the light aimed at the dog's eyes, then took a determined stride forward. Giving another yell, he hurled the rock.

With a yelp, even though the rock thudded harmlessly against the ground, the dog wheeled. His skinny tail between his legs, he scrambled away, claws clicking on the stony surface. Lester ran forward, scooped up the compass, and jerked upright to face the dog again. The creature

stopped at what it seemed to regard as a safe distance, looking back over its bony shoulder. Emboldened, Lester
hurled two more rocks in its direction and watched until the creature fled and disappeared among the distant
shadows.

When Lester attempted to transfer the compass to his
right hand, he found his hands were shaking so that it was
difficult to do. There was a sudden sharp pain in his thumb.
Looking at his hand, and the compass within it, he saw a
trickle of blood run down his wrist. The glass on the compass was shattered and an edge of it had cut him. Trembling, sick with dismay, he managed to secure the instrument in its carrying sheath. Holding it in one hand, the
flash in the other, he started back toward camp, watching
over his shoulder. Even a drop or two of blood on the
ground might be enough for the famished dog to sniff out,
prompting it to overcome its cowardice and attack.

It couldn't smell blood from hundreds of feet away, Lester assured himself. Nevertheless, his spine felt cold as he
ran toward the tents showing as pyramid-shaped blurs in
the distance. Except for the glass cover, the compass was
probably intact, he decided. The dog must have knocked
it from the rock, hoping it might be edible.

At the edge of the campsite Lester slowed his pace, once
more careful to make no noise. A few more minutes and
he was at the tent door. Patrick lay as before, one arm
crooked under his head for a pillow. He stirred when Lester bumped against the center pole, but that was all.

Back in the sleeping bag, Lester lay for a long while
staring at the few stars visible through the tent window,
tensely listening for any sound that would indicate the

presence of the dog, or a dog pack. The night was still, only the small murmur of the stream touching the silence. Should he tell Aunt Zeb about the dog in the morning? If there were any danger, she ought to know. Perhaps he could tell her in such a way that it would not be necessary to reveal his blunder in leaving the compass.

He fell into a troubled sleep and woke, seemingly only short minutes later, to see morning light flooding the tent and a yawning Patrick sitting up in the bag opposite.

"Bacon's frying already," Patrick said. "Smell it? Race you to the frying pan, Les."

Lester grunted. He was in no mood for talking, much less for racing. "Go ahead. I've got a headache—I'll be along in a minute." He stalled until Patrick had left the tent; then he removed the compass from its case and tried to test it. The needle wavered before settling into place, and one tip looked bent. But it was pointing north toward what Lester reckoned was north.

From the cook site came two light blasts on Zebrina's whistle. Lester finished dressing hastily, secured the compass firmly in his hip pocket, and hurried to join the others. Even as he trotted toward them, he slyly inspected the dry ground for some trace of a dog's paw prints. If they were there, he did not see them.

The dishes were done, litter buried, the tents dismantled, and everything loaded once again into the station wagon.

"Now," Zebrina said, righting her wobbly helmet on her grizzled hair, "the countdown. Patrick? Contour maps, repair kit, nylon cord . . ."

Lester waited his turn. When she reached "compass" he nodded but avoided her glance.

"All right then, dears. We're off." She surveyed the campsite with a final, probing gaze, then climbed in behind the steering wheel.

The road was still bad, she found, and it grew progressively worse. After five miles of negotiating treacherous ruts, gullies, and small rockslides, she questioned her own wisdom. She should have left the car at the camp where they could have reclaimed it safely for the journey back. For the road now was narrowed to one lane, becoming a trap. There was no way of turning around on it, and the prospect of backing down the winding miles was not an inviting one.

"We should have brought pack horses," Patrick suggested.

"That would have been a wonderful idea—about a week ago," Sylvie remarked.

Fay pressed her forefinger against a plump cheek, frowning thoughtfully. "I'll vote for a tow truck. Knobs, what do you vote for?"

"She's not voting age yet," Patrick said.

"Pegasus," Knobs asserted with no hesitation. "He's got wings."

"Very good, love," Zeb said approvingly.

"What do you vote for, Lester?" Sylvie asked.

He had scarcely followed the dialogue and was at a loss. "Uh— I don't know. I haven't thought about it."

"What were you thinking about, then?" Fay pressed.

He swallowed. "Wild dogs." He wanted to take the

words back, having meant to tell Zeb in confidence. It was too late. Everybody was looking at him, waiting.

Patrick interposed. "I've thought about them plenty of times. So what?"

"I saw one," Lester said. "Last night."

Sylvie gasped. "When you went on the walk by yourself?"

"Yes—I mean no, not at sunset. It was later. I had to get up in the night and I wandered off a ways, across the road, and there was this wild dog staring at me. Not right near the camp. He was horribly thin. Starving."

Fay put her arms around herself and shivered. Sylvie made a grimace of fear, partly exaggerated.

"Honest?" Patrick said, looking at Lester half in awe.

Knobs was silent, arranging and rearranging her jacks in varying positions.

Aunt Zebrina also was silent, studying Lester's somber eyes in the rear-view mirror. "You should have come and told me, dear."

"There was only one," he answered. "Anyhow, it was more scared than I was. I threw a rock at it and it raced off."

"Did you truly, Lester?" There was admiration in Sylvie's light-blue eyes.

Patrick responded modestly, "I don't know whether I'd have the nerve for that or not." He crossed his sturdy forearms across his chest, looking thoughtful. "Maybe I would though."

"What did it look like?" Fay asked breathlessly. "Was it horrible—with long fangs and a dripping tongue and . . ."

"That's enough of such foolishness," Aunt Zeb cut in. "The poor animal did nobody any harm, and although it would have been wiser if Lester had wakened me, let's hear no more about it. We have more important problems to deal with." As though reinforcing her declaration, the car jolted into a large pothole, shuddered, and then swayed back onto a comparatively level surface. "Squad, I fear I was foolish in continuing on by car. Still, there's nothing to do now but keep going until we can at least find a turn-around spot."

Patrick pointed toward a hill they would have to ascend. "The road looks a lot better over there."

"Yes, it does," Zebrina agreed. In low gear she steered the staggering vehicle and bumping trailer downslope, trying to keep stone bruises to the tires at a minimum, and avoiding rocks that might threaten the car's underbody. Now they had reached the beginning of the upward incline, and the surface was almost smooth.

"We're in luck!" Patrick exclaimed. "For a while, anyhow." He craned upward in his seat, straining to see over the hill's crest. The car topped the rise and they all saw how the highway widened, surprisingly intact except for an occasional bump or ripple.

Zebrina relaxed. Even though they would have to abandon the car eventually, the farther they could journey with it, the better. She glanced at the odometer. They had covered two hundred and twenty miles since leaving Old City. Another twenty, or even less, would put them within striking distance of their goal. She had never counted on making more than two hundred miles in the station wagon, so no matter what happened now, they were ahead of the game. Once near the Lost Lakes Pass, they would have exhausted their gasoline supply, except for the reserve tank that would see them home again.

They rounded a turn which gave them a view of a desolate valley below, and what appeared to be a military complex. Approaching the complex was a line of olive-drab GEMs hovering ten feet above the rocky terrain, a reminder that they were by no means in the wilderness yet. Zebrina took time to glance upward from the road. Still remote, but there, were the Lost Lakes peaks, and the blessedness of great pines, and streams that she was certain would provide potable water. She wagged a forefinger toward the lofty green spears of forest against the blue sky, the towering blocks of shining granite. "Look, Squad."

They leaned and tipped their faces upward to try to glimpse the distant heights.

"Oh, it's beautiful," Fay breathed. "Let's sing something. What shall we sing, Sylvie?"

To everybody's surprise, Knobs, her voice squeaky but not hollow, launched into "The Battle Hymn of the Republic." "Mine eyes have seen the glory of the comin' of the Lord; He is tramplin' out the vintage where the grapes of Ruth are stored. . . ."

"Grapes of *wrath!*" Sylvie said, and giggled.

Fay said hotly, "Don't laugh at her! Anybody can make a mistake. Come on, Knobs, honey, go on, and we'll all join in."

Knobs drew back into her corner, eyes lowered, silent.

"Fay's right, Knobs— Celeste," Zeb said. "You should continue." Silence. "Where in the world did you learn that song, treasure? It's one of my favorites."

Knobs picked up a jack, set it down, then held it again, brooding over it. "At the gospel meetin's," she said finally in so low a voice it was hard for anyone to hear. "Mommy and me and Silver Daddy used to go there. The preacher said it was a sin to gamble. But they did, all the time, any-how."

"What's a gospel meeting, Aunt Zeb?" Fay asked.

"Never mind," Zeb said. "Since you suggested the singing, dear, why don't you start it if Celeste prefers not to go on?"

Fay accepted the invitation eagerly, considering her clear soprano voice one of her few assets. Gaily she began the old folk song, "Mocking Bird Hill." "Tralala, diddle dee, it gives me a thrill, to wake up in the morning on Mocking Bird Hill. . . ."

The rest joined in, even Aunt Zeb with a harmonizing contralto. Lester pretended to sing along but mostly he only shaped the words soundlessly.

They were on the final chorus when Zeb closed her mouth in a silent line that expressed resignation more than surprise. "Well, Squad, I hope your lungs and leg muscles are in good condition."

The group broke off singing and looked ahead to where the road ended in a rockslide as broad and high as a fallen skyscraper.

"Well, there's room to turn around in," Zeb said calmly. "*Just.*"

Patrick flexed his muscles and swelled his chest, peering up at the mountains. "Here we come!" he called to them.

The moment the car stopped, the group piled out eagerly, happy at the prospect of being at the real beginning of their adventure. Even Lester's face became animated.

Everything would be all right, he told himself. Even if the compass didn't work, he knew how to make one—or, rather, he had read about how to make one from an ordinary needle like the one in the Squad's repair kit. There were always other ways to tell direction—the moss on the north side of trees, the sun, the stars. He took a deep breath of the mountain air.

"How high are we?" he asked Aunt Zeb.

"Five thousand feet," she answered without hesitation, for she knew the place well, seeing the edge of a creek-spanning bridge that peeked out from the rockslide. The still-intact rampart of concrete was marked *Lovers' Creek*, the very place where she and James had come on their honeymoon so many years ago. He had not been so much a hunter then as a hiker and fisherman, and they had tramped over every acre of the territory between the creek and the Lost Lakes Pass.

"We'll eat first, dears, and then pack up," Zeb said, as exuberant as they. She felt secure, almost young, and ready to test herself against the slopes, the trees, and the sky.

# CHAPTER 9

THE land rose abruptly under their feet as the Squad,
Zebrina in the lead, climbed upward. Zeb set the pace, one
which at first had seemed frustratingly slow to the young
people. Everyone except Knobs, who clung nervously close
to Zebrina, had wasted energy darting off at frequent intervals to investigate anything of interest along the trail. Now,
after two hours of climbing, there were no such activities,
and very little talk.

Here and there were a few scattered trees, but still not
the forest the Squad had looked forward to. Encouragingly,
however, they began to find clumps of vegetation in fissures
in the rock, and occasional gleams of moss. But for the most
part, even when they reached six thousand feet, the landscape remained ravaged. Ancient mining shafts and old
water wheels were mixed in with much later developments.
Where once in the 1980s a molybdenum mine had flour-
ished, rusting bulldozers stood like the brown skeletons of
vanished animals, the land around them stripped of anything living. Drilling rigs and the remains of a helicopter
lay on the raw slope amid the stumps of what had once
been a magnificently forested mountain.

The forest grandeur, or what remained of it, was still above the Squad, and all kept their eyes trained on the still unreached greenness. Fay, especially, yearned toward the tree shadows above, visualizing a resting place by a bright stream. Increasingly her extra poundage bore down upon her, and she envied both Knobs and Sylvie, their bodies seemingly weightless in the thinning air. If only Aunt Zeb would call a rest halt soon. But Zeb, in spite of her age and swollen ankles, trudged on, breathing swiftly though steadily, keeping up a measured pace.

Behind Fay came Patrick and then Lester, and when Fay glanced back at times she saw that they seemed nowhere near as fatigued as she. Patrick's cheeks were red, of course, but they always were. Lester, on his long, thin legs, seemed to have time to look around everywhere except at the vague trail. Once, Zeb had said, the trail had been almost a thoroughfare. Now it was so indistinct that Fay marveled at how Zeb could follow it, for it was only a slightly depressed, zigzag course between the leafless rocks. Fay concentrated on keeping up with Sylvie and Knobs, counting her steps.

"Mountain climbing," Zebrina had instructed them, "requires a steady pace, not sudden spurts and long halts. Breathe through your mouths, dears, even pant if you must, but keep up the steady pace, neither fast nor slow."

Fay had almost given up hope of any surcease when she spied a tall, spreading Jeffrey pine above, its sweeping branches providing a broad mantle of shade.

Behind her, Patrick exclaimed, "There's a place to rest, Aunt Zeb! Look at the size of that pine."

So Patrick was eager to rest, too, Fay thought, relieved.

Aunt Zeb stopped and looked back over her small regiment. She was puffing from her exertions, perspiration trickling down her temples, moisture stains under her armpits, but there was vigor in her stance and voice. She shifted her knapsack higher on her shoulders. "Yes, love, I see it. If we must stop there, we will, but roughly fifteen minutes from here there's a delightful brook—or once was—in a thick stand of Jeffrey and ponderosa. If you prefer to rest here, we'll take a vote. I recommend, Squad, that we toil on."

Feeling doomed, Fay listened to Sylvie, Patrick, Lester, and Knobs vote to go on.

"Go on," she echoed feebly, and found herself counting each laborious step again as the trail wound ever more steeply upward. She was lagging behind the leaders now, so much so that she was impeding Lester and Patrick.

"Why don't you two go ahead?" she panted.

"We're supposed to keep the line of march," Patrick said.

Lester shrugged. "No hurry, anyway. This isn't rush-hour traffic."

"I don't want to be an obstacle," Fay said.

"We're all together in this," Patrick said, then moved up toward her and held out his hand. "Do you want me to carry your canteen?"

Fay wrestled with temptation. It was astonishing how heavy the two-quart container had become. Its strap abraded her shoulder, along with all the other trappings she carried. Her reply surprised her. "Thanks," she said, "but why should you? I'm perfectly capable of carrying my own weight."

"Well, there's plenty of it," Patrick said and laughed. Immediately he looked sorry. "I mean, we all have lots to carry."

Her cheeks burning, Fay strode onward. He was perfectly hateful, she thought. Of course, she had left herself open with her stupid remark. Still, he was hateful. And he wasn't the most slender person in the world himself. Her resentment gave her fresh energy and she climbed on with new vigor, so clutched by her thoughts of hateful Patrick that she almost forgot the ordeal of exertion and was surprised when she heard Zeb call out, "Halt!"

Fay sprawled in the shade of the pines with the others, lifting her canteen to her mouth. There was a slight wind, enough to make a murmuring sound among the glistening pine needles, and there was also the sound of the brook that Zeb had promised. Pine cones lay on the ground nearby, and there were some swatches of grass, weeds, and a few small, struggling plants that Fay could not name.

Zebrina scarcely paused to rest as she rushed from one green spot to another. "Oh, look, dears, that's a valiant sulphur flower there—the buckwheat family, you know!" Though she had stripped off her pack, her canteen and various other articles dangled from her shoulders and waist. She knelt down. "Old-man's-beard—or golden groundsel. Two plants! Of course, they won't bloom until about August, if they ever do. But think of the promise, the wonderful chance!" Suddenly she lay down, flat on her back, staring up at the sky, her glasses sparkling as if reflecting the excitement in her eyes. "Trees, wind song, and wild flowers!"

Knobs sat cross-legged in the shade of a young yellow

pine, the bones of her knees seeming to thrust through her sunburned skin. "I thought it would be different," she said in a voice that was familiarly hollow. "I thought we'd find the animals by now." With an obvious look of disappointment, she glanced at the plants Zeb had exclaimed over. "They ain't nearly as pretty as the lemon tree."

Zeb did not unfasten her gaze from the sky, but said gently, "Perhaps not, treasure, but they are miracles. Our lemon tree is a domestic, indulged plant. These out here, Celeste, are miracles."

"What's a miracle?" Knob asked.

"Life," Aunt Zeb said. She sat up, drank from her canteen, then lay down again, turning on her side and resting her head against her elbow. "Patrick, wake me in ten minutes, at which time we shall resume our endeavors."

Patrick, slumped on a half-rotted log, looked dutifully at his wrist watch, noting the exact second. "Right," he said. Almost at once, he and the others heard Zebrina's deep breathing in sleep. Patrick shook his head in wonder and grinned at Fay, showing his broad white teeth. "She's as good as Napoleon. He could sleep any time he wanted to, even in the middle of a crucial battle."

Fay struggled between her hurt feelings and her desire to have Patrick's good will. "I didn't know that about Napoleon," she admitted.

"Lots of people don't," Patrick said.

Lester was squatted on his heels, inspecting lichen on Patrick's log. "He was a power-mad supermurderer," he said with contempt. "The reason he could sleep at will was because he had no conscience whatsoever."

Patrick bristled. "He was a great general, just the same."

"Sh-h-h," Sylvie cautioned, pointing toward Aunt Zeb. Sylvie had dragged the butterfly net out of her bedroll and sat trying to relace the raveled strings.

Lester walked off toward the brook. He bent down and stroked the cold water over his forearms. He was tempted to drink it, as the water in the canteens was tepid, but he did not. Aunt Zeb would undoubtedly test the brook's purity before they hiked on.

From where he stood, he could see the high mountain forest beyond, stands of mountain hemlock and white pine. In one section there was a long, wide swath of fallen trees, as if a giant scythe had been swung against them. It was the track of a sonic boom, he realized, and wondered how many such trails of destruction marred the wilderness fly routes. Higher yet were the gnarled and naked peaks above timber line. Up there somewhere were the bristlecone pines, the oldest living trees in the world. He had seen pictures of them, twisted and stunted giants thousands of years old. Zeb had said nothing about going there. It would, in fact, be like returning to the dead lower levels, for up at twelve thousand feet, only the hardiest plants could grow on the wind-scoured heights.

He studied the stream closely, watching for some sign of animal life, a frog, a trout, even a dragonfly. There were a fishline and a hook in the emergency kit, and he wondered if any of them would ever need to use it. He could not imagine himself killing anything, even at the risk of starvation. Nor had he ever caught a fish in his life, though the artificial trout pond in New City was only a block from his house. Wandering slowly back toward the others, he thought about the gun which Zeb had brought along and which she carried strapped to her pack frame. He hated the sight of it, as he did that of guns of any kind. His father had given him a .22 as a Christmas gift and had insisted on instructing him in its use. Lester had proved to be a good marksman, for all his revulsion.

Before he rejoined the others, he removed the compass from his pocket. Facing what he believed was north, he tested the instrument. The needle wavered and when it finally settled into place it pointed in what was evidently an eastern direction. Lester gritted his teeth, then had the reassuring thought that perhaps minerals in the rock formations had a magnetic attraction that caused the problem. He tucked the compass back into place and reached the others just as Patrick called out to Aunt Zeb, "Ten minutes!"

She opened her eyes, sat up, and shook herself. "Ah, that was wonderful. I feel like a new woman." She groped for her glasses, which she had tucked into a pocket of her knapsack, hooked them firmly over her ears, and stood up. "Hand me the map, Patrick." He held it out and she studied it. "Minaret Summit, Laurel Canyon, Devil's Postpile—um, a pity we can't take in the Postpile. It's a geologic wonder but we'd have to wade through pumice dust to our ankles, with no forest cover. The thing to do, I think —yes, definitely—is to continue on toward Big Lost Lake. Remember, if by any chance we become separated, the lake has a huge rock tower some twenty miles west of it, Crystal Crag, a resistant granitic rock around which flowed the two arms of a glacier. It's a remnant of a once-high ridge that separated the drainages of Crystal Lake and— Oh, well, never mind. Meet at the Crag. Let's see if we can freshen our canteens from the brook."

At the water's edge she went through the testing routine, then raised an exuberant face. "Beautiful! Eighty-percent-pure mountain water, my dears. Fill up."

Once the canteens were filled, Zeb strode back to the trail. She bent down over the one sulphur-flower plant and the two sprigs of groundsel, sighing with delight before she straightened, adjusted her pack straps, and faced the almost-invisible trail ahead. "If I've reckoned correctly, Hawk's Pass is only a mile from here. On your mark, Squad." She lifted her right hand, firing an imaginary starting gun, and started off.

They had covered a half mile, the trail winding between giant boulders left over from glacial times, when Sylvie cried out "Oh!" and leaped from the path. As she ran she struggled to extricate the butterfly net from her pack, her eyes fixed on the trunk of a large Jeffrey pine. Something brilliantly blue fluttered there. Immediately she knew what it was. A blue swallowtail! She would capture it and, when she got home, show it to her father. He would buy a case for it and have it standing right beside his own specimen case. He would look down at not one blue swallowtail, but two, amazed and proud.

She paused, feet sliding on the pine-needle-carpeted ground, then went closer. It couldn't be a butterfly. The shape wasn't right. But the color was, that radiant blue, and that flapping motion. She stared and bit her lip, dismay a round, hard shape in her throat as if she had swallowed a rock. The beautiful butterfly was nothing more than a scrap of torn blue plastic that had caught on the rough bark and become permanently wedged in a crevice. In spite of rain and snow it had kept its color through the years it had hung there. A scrap of some long-ago child's lost kite, she wondered, or a fragment of some vanished camper's air mattress? It did not matter. It was a brilliant blue lie—like her own dream of a blue swallowtail.

She turned away and saw the others staring at her from a distance, though Aunt Zeb was approaching, anticipation in her face. "What is it, treasure?"

Sylvie studied the ground, her lower lip unsteady. "Nothing. I thought I saw something real. It was only . . ." She coughed against the stiffness of her throat, then pointed toward the tree.

Zebrina squinted and saw the blue scrap for what it was. She put her arm around Sylvie's shoulders. "Well, sweetheart, at least you had your eyes open. And you had the joy of the illusion. I've been visually deceived a hundred times, thinking a red pop can in a ditch was a rose." She gave a small, self-deriding chuckle. "Yes, I've been fooled time and time again but, you know, for a blind instant red or orange pop cans in the weeds gave me the same esthetic response as a glimpse of poppies—until I realized what a dupe I was. Beauty is in the eye of the beholder, dear." Gently she propelled Sylvie back toward the trail.

Knobs, who had tagged after Zeb, met them halfway. She studied Sylvie with a look of knowingness in her pale-lashed eyes. "You thought you were gonna catch somethin', didn't you? I seen you get your net out." Her gaze was frank and open, not derisive, but Sylvie felt raw to any questioning.

"I only went to look at something more closely," she snapped. She pulled free from Aunt Zeb's embracing arm and took her position on the trail again, her chin high, trying to ignore the two boys and Fay.

Silently the group proceeded on its way again, dusty Hawk's Pass directly ahead.

It was nearing sunset when they began searching for a meadow Zeb had chosen for their night's rest. They followed what was left of an old dirt road through a windwashed forest, passing hills formed by ancient volcanic cones. At one point, the stone foundations of a miner's cabin peeked out of the underbrush. And often they saw the crumbling remains of mine tunnels, decaying timbers, bits of machinery, and rusted tram cars.

The wind had strengthened during the afternoon, and dark clouds had brushed the sunlight. Now, at sunset, the clouds were blacker, with burnished rims. Then, abruptly, the sunlight faded and gloom descended as if a vast curtain had been lowered. It was at almost exactly that moment that Zebrina stopped and called, "Halt." She peered through the gloom, her index finger pointing stiffly ahead. "We've reached the crack—come close, Squad, but watch your step. It's well worth our while to pause and take a look."

"Crack?" Patrick said, feeling apprehension but forcing himself to walk warily to where Aunt Zeb stood. He followed her pointing finger and saw the long, narrow opening in the earth. It was a black and seemingly bottomless scar, Jeffrey pines growing from its upper edges.

"An earthquake's souvenir," Aunt Zeb said. "Not a true

fault, however, but very ancient. In the old days, Lost Lakes residents used it as a refrigerator, for its depths, even in summer, are full of snow. See, there it glimmers."

Patrick felt faintly giddy. Heights bothered him, though he tried to deny this weakness in himself. He forced himself to creep closer to the gap and stare down into its snow-shrouded blackness. He had experienced slight earth tremors in New City but he had never seen the earth cracked open. Looking now at the jagged, gaping split in the earth's surface, he imagined himself falling forever between the terrible, slanting walls. He drew back, the stable earth seeming to quiver under his feet. Alongside Zeb, the others were peering down into the crack with seemingly calm fascination—except for Knobs. She stood at a distance, lonely, huddled inside her own skin, her fingers exploring her lips in a mindless, fearful gesture. Then suddenly she sat down, pulled her jacks and ball from her pocket, and frantically cleared a circle of ground for her game.

Her nose was running, Patrick saw. Snot-nose, he thought, but he squatted down beside her, silent, and offered her his handkerchief.

"On your mark!" Aunt Zeb prompted, turning away from the earth gap. "Knobs, dear, pick up your jacks quickly. We may be in for a storm, and we've some distance yet to go."

The storm struck before they found the meadow. They were in a welter of rocks and lashing trees.

"I'm sorry, darlings," Zebrina said as they hurried toward the shelter of a wide, overhanging roof of lava, "but I'm afraid we've missed the meadow for the night. Perhaps we're in luck, with this handy rock shelter. How do you vote? Shall we push on or take what fate provides?"

There was an ominous soreness on Fay's heel. In spite of Aunt Zeb's warning to wear only thoroughly broken-in shoes, she had worn ones that were still creaky-new. She wanted desperately to stay in the shelter of the rock ledge but she dared not voice her opinion until the others had.

"I vote to stay," Lester said.

"Stay," Patrick and the others echoed.

"Stay it is, then," Zeb said, drawing back from the splashing rain. "In the morning we'll take our bearings with the help of the compass, since we seem to have lost the trail—or else it has been obliterated by time as well as darkness. Perhaps we'll arise to a brilliant sky. Storms, my dears, are also part of life." She glanced around her at the cavelike shelter. "Who knows what lovely wild things once may have sought refuge here, even as we do. A beautiful lioness and her cubs—and, long before that, human ancestors." She turned, meaning to relieve herself of her knapsack and rifle, but in the process her head knocked sharply against the low overhang of rock. The pith helmet flew from her head and something flashed through the air, then crashed with a brittle sound.

The Squad stared, horror-eyed, at the sight of Aunt Zeb standing before them, hand to her forehead, her glasses missing. As in a tennis match when all heads turn in the direction of a serve or a return, their heads turned simultaneously and their eyes fixed on the broken eyeglasses on the cave floor. The shatterproof lenses were intact but the nosepiece had cracked completely in two. No one moved.

"Patrick—somebody—find my glasses, please!" There was an edge of panic in Zeb's voice.

Lester stooped down and picked up the separate halves of the broken frames. He held them up. "Here, only . . ."

"Oh, thank you, love," she said, reaching out. She paused, peering at what was in his hands. Her face working, she groped for both halves of the spectacles, then with fumbling fingers pressed the two parts together as if they could be magically welded by her will power alone. "Well —well, dears . . . We mustn't be upset. We'll just have to tape them together somehow, that's all." Her voice trailed off weakly while she stared through the gloom.

"Sure!" Partick responded heartily. "There's adhesive tape in the medical kit. We'll fix them for you, Auntie Zeb."

In a moment, he and Lester were bent over the task. A frown appeared on Patrick's face, sweat on Lester's upper lip. Finally, Patrick looked toward Zeb, his eyes swimming with apology. "The tape doesn't stick very well—and there's a piece of the bridge missing, so they're all wobbly."

The children watched as Zeb tried to fit the sagging frames in place. "That should do, I'm sure," Zeb said, but her fingers were trembling as she attempted to hold the eyeglasses steady. Suddenly she sat down, both hands in her lap, the glasses sagging uselessly against her cheeks.

Zebrina sighed deeply, staring at a vague heap of rocks across the cave. Everything was blurred—and her spare glasses were miles away, back in the glove compartment of the station wagon.

The Squad waited for her to speak, their faces pale in

the dimness, glancing at each other in chagrin and even fear.

The cave was illuminated briefly by a bolt of lightning. Then came the round roll of thunder.

"I'm scared," Knobs whimpered, moving close to Zeb.

Fumbling, Zeb put her arm around the child's shoulders. "There's nothing to fear, love. We're safely out of the rain and wind. Patrick, you find some tinder and dry wood, if possible. Lester, you can help with the flash and the Electro-lantern. Sylvie, dear, get out the food packets. Fay . . ." her voice wandered off. "The pans, et cetera."

In spite of their training, nobody moved. They remained staring at their almost-sightless leader.

Zebrina removed her useless glasses, an angry flush mottling her face. "Have you forgotten how to perform your duties? This is no time to stand and stare! I may be a stupid and forgetful old woman, but I am not entirely helpless. Now, hurry and use your young legs and bright eyes and prepare this camp for the night."

Everyone except Sylvie immediately began unloading gear in preparation for the various chores. Sylvie remained looking fixedly at Zebrina. "But what are you—what will we do now?"

"We shall do whatever we have to do, Sylvie. There will be no decisions tonight. Sufficient unto the day is the evil thereof." Zeb clamped her lips together and proceeded silently to unpack her own gear, operating by feel as much as by sight. A flicker of lightning threw her shadow against the rock wall behind her, giant-sized head and shoulders, with Knobs's jerky and smaller shadow behind hers.

"We'll have a fire going fast," Patrick spoke from the dripping edge of the shelter, his rain cape already on, his camp ax in hand.

"I know you will, dear," Zeb said, her voice gentle again. She gazed toward him and only Fay was in a position to see the frustration in the straining eyes.

"Poor Auntie Zeb," she whispered to Sylvie as together they moved a dry bench of rock that would serve as a work space.

"Poor us," Sylvie responded.

# CHAPTER 10

AGAIN, Lester did not sleep well. Aunt Zeb was counting on fixing their location with the help of the compass in the morning. But was the compass dependable? If not, he must warn her, no matter how humiliating it would be. Or would it be better to say nothing in order not to alarm the Squad more than they already were? There was a way to use an ordinary old-fashioned wrist watch or pocket watch as a fairly reliable compass, but the digital watches the Squad used lacked old-style dials, the hours, minutes, and seconds showing through a small window in the timepiece.

Although Lester's head was under the shelter of the rock roof, rain splashed against the foot of his sleeping bag, the wind threatening to tear off the waterproof cape he had tried to secure there. Patrick, beside him, was undoubtedly receiving a soaking too. Zebrina and the girls had the drier portion of the shelter. Against the wall, at a safe distance from the sleeping bags, the embers of the night's fire still crackled and gave off a crimson glow.

To confess about the compass, or not to confess . . . It was no time of night to play Hamlet, Lester chided himself. He struggled to remember some appropriate instruction from Sri Krishna. *He who does the task dictated by duty, caring nothing for the fruit of the action, he is a yogi . . .*

But I care for the fruit of my action, Lester fretted. The broken compass is the fruit of my inaction. He ground his teeth silently. He could never be a yogi. He would be a blundering idiot all of his life, a disgrace in his own eyes, a tragic disappointment to his parents. He continued to stare at the fire and then, in spite of his mental anguish, slept.

It was then that Patrick propped himself up on his elbows and took his turn at watching the rain on one side, the fire on the other. He had been well aware of Lester's wakefulness but had said nothing, preoccupied with his own problems. Whether the Squad went on in the morning or tried to retrace their steps, it would be he, Patrick, who would have to lead. Aunt Zeb would have all she could do to follow, with Knobs or someone else as her guide. He felt less potential as a hero now that he was confronted with a crisis, and yet he held visions of himself proving his worth. He was definitely the strongest and steadiest, he told himself. The fainting episode had been a freak thing, like his inward chill at the sight of the earthquake crack. He would make out. He must.

The morning world glistened with wetness but a pale sun shone through lingering clouds. Zebrina was the first up and had managed to drag in fresh fuel for the fire, with the help of Knobs, so that the rock shelter blazed with warmth as the others crawled out of their cloth cocoons. Water was already boiling for their instant cereal. Best of all, Zeb seemed to have recovered her cheerfulness and vigor. Even so, the group sat eating their breakfasts with an attitude of suspense, waiting for what she would say.

Not until everything was tidied up, all packs and other gear in order, did she speak. She stood before them, the helmet back in place, pack slung over her shoulders. Only the familiar dark-rimmed glasses were missing.

"Squad," she announced, "you recall that I said earlier that we might very well make this a brief camping trip of two or three days. We are at an altitude, and in terrain, where we should have seen animals by now, if there are any. Regardless of the accident to my glasses, it would seem pointless to go on. We have found some encouraging signs, after all—some grass and living weeds, a pure brook, a mosquito, and two species of wild flowers. That should be reward enough. Now, the sensible thing is to make our way back down the trail. I am sorry, but that is my studied conclusion."

The members of the Squad looked at each other. Almost always, before, Zeb had put matters to a vote. Now she was already busy making her last-minute arrangements for departure.

"Knobs, dear, fetch me my canteen." She walked warily toward the edge of the shelter, one hand above her head to warn her of any threatening rock projection. "Lester, let's take a compass reading. According to my reckoning, we should aim northeast from here to recover the trail."

Lester fumbled at his hip pocket, his hands sweating.

Patrick, looking dejected, stood gazing morosely at the ground.

Knobs trotted toward Zeb with the canteen, tears sliding down her pointed face. "If we go back, we won't ever find Pegasus!"

"Who?" Sylvie asked.

Knobs drew back behind Zebrina, chin tucked down against the front of her blouse, a spot of pink on each cheek, a wary look in her eyes. "Nothin'," she said.

"I know who Pegasus is," Fay spoke up, proud in her knowledge. "It's in Grecian mythology. It's a horse with wings that can fly all over the sky."

"Where else would anything fly?" Sylvie remarked. To Knobs she said, "You'd never find Pegasus, anyhow, because he's a figment of the imagination."

"I—I would so!" Knobs stuttered.

"Anyway," Patrick cut in, "maybe if we kept going on up another thousand feet or so we'd really know about the animals. Not Pegasus, but real ones. You said yourself, Aunt Zeb . . ."

"Patrick, love, don't remind me of what I said. We are going to go back down. I am sorry but I am responsible for your welfare, all of you. Let's have no more wrangling. Now, Lester, the compass." He held it toward her in an unsteady hand. "No, no, dear, you'll have to take the reading."

"Oh, sure," he said and held the instrument in his palm, staring at it as blindly as if his eyesight were no better than Zebrina's. "I'm not sure," he murmured, watching the erratic needle. "It's quivery—I mean, I can't be certain. All the mineral deposits around here. . ." He glanced away from the untrustworthy compass, relying on the position of the sun, secretly trying to study the moss on

the trunks of some nearby trees. With an attempt at
authority, he pointed, stating, "Northeast should be directly toward that dark cliff on the right." In the middle
of his sentence, his changing voice broke in the manner he
loathed, yodeling up into a squeak.

"Should be, or *is?*" Zeb challenged, bending her face
close to the compass. "Yes, I can make out the needle—but
what's wrong with the glass?" She moved an exploratory
forefinger toward it.

"It's—it got broken. I must have bumped against something." Lester writhed with self-contempt at his deceit.
But he was certain that his sense of direction was correct.

"No matter," Zeb said. "As long as you keep the metal
lid closed, the needle won't be affected." She drew herself
up. "Everyone ready? Northeast, then, toward the cliff.
Once we are back on the trail, we'll be safe. Even though
I may have some difficulty seeing it, I can feel its direction
with my feet." She took a firm stride forward, then halted.
"Patrick, you lead the way." She reached for Knobs's hand.

Proud at being the leader, but disappointed to be in
charge of a retreat, Patrick stepped to the front. He put his
shoulders back, faced ahead, and ordered, "March!"

As he recalled their arrival the night before, he remembered that they had descended to seek for the rock-bordered
meadow Zeb had described. So now the path should lead
upward, as it did after only some hundred feet. He fixed
his eyes on the distant cliff, concentrating on it as if it
were a living thing that could suddenly lurch out of sight.

The way grew steeper. At one side of their trackless
course a jumble of buildings appeared, or what had been
buildings. A huge, ornate fireplace chimney stood intact,

and a crumbling concrete oval that must once have been a swimming pool. Beyond, blackly silhouetted against the sky, were the twisted ruins of a ski lift.

The ruins were apparently those of some large recreation development, Patrick thought, one of many that had dotted the region years ago. He looked back, trying to ascertain whether or not he was setting too fast a pace. Perhaps. Zeb was obviously having a difficult time on the increasingly stony path. He saw her stumble over a rock and rest one hand heavily on Knobs's shoulder as she caught her balance.

"We're not too far from the cliff now, Auntie Zeb," he called to her. "Shall we take a break when we reach there?"

"Only long enough to take our bearings again, dear."

The sun had disappeared once more, hidden behind a thick, dark-gray overcast.

It could snow in the higher altitudes, Patrick thought as he trudged on. But not very likely at the six or seven thousand feet the Squad had reached, and the rest of the way they should be going downhill. They were certainly not descending now, he observed, his shoes slipping on the steepness of the grade. The dark cliff was still in view but seemed farther off than before. He hesitated, wondering if he should consult Zeb, then forged onward. What kind of leader paused and asked his followers the proper path? Anyhow, there was no real danger. Certainly not from wild animals.

There was a spatter of rain, a flash of sunlight, and then gloomy overcast again. The mountain peaks above timber line, some of them eleven and twelve thousand feet

high, were silvered with glaciers and snow. Patrick tried
to identify the peaks from his memory of Zeb's maps—
Bloody Mountain, Laurel, Mammoth.

Abruptly the path descended, bringing relief to his
climbing muscles. Again he glanced back. The others followed closely behind, in tight formation.

"Looks like we're entering a canyon," he said, more to
himself than to the others, his voice lost among the scuffing
noise of boot soles and displaced stones. Tall ferns brushed
his knees, and the wet trees dripped cold raindrops down
his back. It was almost like being down at the bottom of
the earthquake crack, he thought. He paused, disconcerted,
realizing that the cliff landmark was nowhere in view.
Well, that was to be expected; it couldn't show through
the steep canyon walls. The path seemed to rise ahead.
Once out of the canyon, the way would surely be clear.

He went on, trying vainly to find the position of the
cloud-obscured sun, when Zeb called, "Halt!" She faced
away from Patrick toward Lester at the rear. "This seems
a *cul-de-sac*, Squad. Lester, let's try the compass again."

He came toward her, a wound shining red on one bare
knee where it had been scraped by a rock.

"Darling, you've hurt yourself!" Zebrina exclaimed,
peering at him. "You have the medicine kit. . . ."

"It doesn't matter," Lester said, interrupting her
brusquely in a way that was not like him. "What does matter is—" He swallowed, the Adam's apple in his thin throat
bobbing, his amber eyes seeming rust-colored in the damp
gloom. He did not bother to remove the compass from his
pocket. "We can't trust the compass, Aunt Zeb. You see,
I left it on a rock. . . ." Swiftly, scarcely allowing time for

a breath, he told her what had happened the night he had seen the wild dog. "I should have told you then, before we got into this mess." He turned his head to avoid Patrick's astonished gaze.

Zeb drew her hand slowly across her mouth, tugged at one large earlobe, and studied the ground as if it held something of remarkable interest. "Yes, dear, you should have. However, that's all beside the point now."

"It says in my survival book," Sylvie volunteered, "that if you find a stream and follow it down, you're bound to reach a road or a settlement."

"Unless the stream goes underground," Patrick said. "Or around and around in circles and through ravines, so that you wear yourself out trying to follow it."

"But the book says . . ." Sylvie started to defend herself.

Zebrina sat down on a convenient boulder, then craned her head back, searching the sky. "We started northeast, yes, but we are now traveling, I judge, almost straight west. Though we are in a temporary declivity we have been gaining, not losing, altitude."

Lester wiped gems of perspiration from his upper lip. "Perhaps—I could try to get back to the car and find your spare glasses, and then . . ."

Zeb merely shook her head.

Knobs hovered near her, gazing anxiously at her. "Are we lost, Auntie Zeb? *Are* we?" Her voice ended on a shrill note, terror lurking in the bones of her face.

"No, no, treasure. Or, even if we were for a time, it would be simply an adventure. We have plenty of food, water, and courage." She casually removed her helmet and ran her hand through her tousled hair. "There's nothing to harm us, after all, except our own fears or stupidity. As long as we are strong and stout of heart . . ."

"There!" Lester exclaimed. "See there!" He raised one hand slowly to point.

"Wha—" Fay started to say, then clapped her hand over her mouth.

In a pale puddle of sunlight, directly beneath a slim red fir, stood an animal. It was a small creature, light yellowish-brown above, with lighter under parts and round ears. It stood up on its haunches, stiffly erect, whiskers shining, forelegs pressed closely against its chest, short tail pointing out behind it.

Nobody spoke and for what seemed a full minute the little animal stood there, alert, listening, a brilliant eye shining in his profile. Suddenly he dived out of sight.

Knobs stood with her usually tight mouth wide open. "Oh-h-h!" she breathed. And then again, "Oh."

"What was it, Aunt Zeb?" Fay whispered, her dark eyes wide.

Patrick, unable to restrain himself, trotted toward the spot where the animal had been, searching for its hideout.

Zebrina kept looking toward the spot. The little figure had been dim to her but it was so familiar a form that there could be no mistake. "A Belding ground squirrel, Squad," she said softly, excitement rippling her voice. " 'Picket pins,' everybody used to call them, dear little creatures that once popped up on every mountain meadow or flat, guarding their holes like furry sentries. Think of it, loves! A living, breathing ground squirrel." The color along her cheekbones was like roses. She looked toward the sky and in the gray-blue firmament imagined that she saw the squirrel's predator, a hawk floating on tilted wings. Not that she wished to see the charming rodent clasped in the hawk's claws, but only that now there was a better chance that hawk wings still cleft the air currents. Mosquito, bat, frog, turtle—ground squirrel, fox, hawk—the chain of life required all the individual links from lowest to highest.

Knobs stood twisting a hand in a lock of hair. "It must of flew away, didn't it, Zeb? It went so fast I couldn't hardly see its wings."

"Oh, honey," Fay blurted, "squirrels don't have wings." Seeing the crushed look on Knobs's face, she appealed to Zeb. "They don't, do they?"

Zebrina kneaded a swollen ankle, pondering, torn between scientific fact and the beseeching look in Knobs's fanatic eyes. "Not as a rule, no, dear. But I have found in life that there are exceptions to everything—and, further, we have to remember that things are far different in the world today. If you study the various evolutionary theories," she went on, being deliberately obscure, if only to bore her listening audience, "you will find that occasional sports, or mutations, do occur. Consider the flying squirrel, so called, with its skin flaps that resemble but are not wings. It is certainly possible that our Belding squirrel has mutated —Knobs may have seen something that I, in my present infirmity, missed."

Knobs's eyes were fixed on Zebrina, brow scrunched together in perplexed attention. "It had wings, all right," she declared firmly.

Patrick sniffed, and Sylvie and Fay exchanged a sly grin, but nobody said anything. Having seen one living wild animal, even one once so commonplace as the ground squirrel, they felt it was not worth arguing about.

The spirits of all had been revived, and when Zeb rose from her resting place, saying confidently, "Lead on, Patrick," the group fell into place and strode onward through the winding canyon toward an ascent approaching a sun-stippled rim of rock.

Sylvie skipped beside Fay, jaunty, one hand ready to seize the protruding handle of her butterfly net. Even Lester, spiritless and humiliated a short while before, raised his head and walked with a fresh spring in his stride.

Fay, too, felt better, almost enough so to ignore the increasing soreness of her heel where her shoe rubbed it over and over. The Quick-band she had surreptitiously applied last night had helped, but now she felt it sliding out of place.

I can stand it, she told herself. I have to. And I'm losing pounds every mile. The folks won't know me when I reach home.

They attained the rock rim and then a stony summit. Patrick attained the prominence first. Soon the others crowded around him.

"At least now, out of that canyon, we can see where we are," Patrick said, looking around at the peaks spread out before them.

Zebrina could make out only the most obvious, and many of those seemed dim. "Can you locate Crystal Crag?" she asked. "It's unmistakable, like a gigantic gray thumb."

Patrick scanned the horizon from one direction to the other, wishing that his eyes were drills that could bore through the mist and overcast and the occasional sun glitter. He shook his head and then, realizing that Aunt Zeb might not be able to see the gesture, said, "No." He drew in his breath, removed his cap, and brushed one hand over his various cowlicks. "I don't know where we are, Aunt Zeb."

Lester cradled his long limbs in a rock trough as if in a familiar armchair. There was an ecstatic look on his face. "There's a rainbow! See it, over that sharpest peak. Let's follow that!"

Patrick flashed a look of disgust in Lester's direction. From broken compass to rainbow in one happy leap, he thought, then asserted his leadership. "We'll take a break here and eat," he declared, "before considering our next step."

He looked at Zebrina from the corner of his eye, while his stomach growled with hunger. She gave a nod and smiled her approval.

# CHAPTER 11

THE rifle seemed a completely useless article to have brought, Zebrina thought, as the group wound upward through thickening lodgepole pines. Some of the tallest and oldest trees were dead, but young ones crowded the forest floor, shouldering their way up toward sunlight. Better an extra compass, and certainly extra glasses, instead of the encumbering gun. Then, impatient with her own regrets—even more useless than the rifle—she determined to make a fresh effort to seek for familiar landmarks. During the last rest stop she had discovered that by cupping her hands around her eyes as though peering through binoculars, she could improve her vision to a considerable extent. It was a strange and exciting discovery, and she wondered what her oculist would say about it. Very likely he would only laugh and call it her imagination. So much for him, she thought indignantly, already holding an imaginary argument with the young doctor. There were many things he did not know yet, for all his brash self-confidence.

"Watch out, Auntie Zeb," Knobs said, giving her hand an extra tug. "There's a rock in the path."

"Thank you, love," Zeb said, making out the object and

sidestepping it. "You're a wonderful help to me, Celeste." Even with her faulty vision she could see the flush of pride in Knobs's small face. Almost from the moment Knobs had started leading her, the child's demeanor had changed, as if for the first time in her life she felt that she had some value to the world. It was almost worth her accident, Zeb consoled herself, as long as the group had no really serious problem in finding their way back to the car.

What they were traveling now was very definitely a path. A deer path, she would have called it in the old days, and even now she could call it nothing else even though there had been no sign of a deer anywhere, so far. Still, in the night there had been a crackling sound as of some heavy animal walking through the wet underbrush, and Sylvie had said she spied a bird that could have been a blue jay. Or more blue plastic, Zeb thought, pitying Sylvie's obsession with finding a butterfly. It would be almost more than Zeb could bear to have the child actually capture any such winged miracle, and yet how could she intervene? Where did one draw the line between human needs and the well-being of nonhuman lives?

She grimaced, reflecting that she had spent half her life in such idle speculations, testing one value against another, fretting over questions more properly left to philosophers, although many philosophers had left things in a greater mess than they had found them. And what grouches some of them were. That old, sour Schopenhauer, berating all womankind. As if anybody would have wanted to marry that misanthrope. And then poor, self-tormenting Kierkegaard. . . .

Zeb clicked her teeth. What on earth was she doing,

mulling over such things at a time like this! It was a wonder she hadn't forgotten a dozen things beside spare glasses.

"Patrick," she said to his back, "when we reach another open promontory, let's make an earnest attempt to identify the peaks. They can't hide their identities from us forever, and I'm increasingly certain that we are taking a very roundabout way to our goal."

"All ri—" Patrick started to say and then stopped. "Hey! There's a track. Two of them. Right on the trail! Here, Aunt Zeb!"

Although Zeb could see Patrick clearly enough, she permitted Knobs to lead her to the spot. Zeb hunched over, squinting down the length of her nose, cupping a hand around one eye. "I knew it!" she exclaimed. "It *is* a deer trail." She continued to stare at the tracks imprinted in the rain-moist earth: neat, clear marks in the shape of cleft hearts. As the others ran forward, she cautioned, "Don't trample them, darlings. Just look and marvel."

Knobs looked up at Zeb. "What kind of marks do a horse's hoofs make?"

"Larger, dear. And if they are shod they have the shape of a—well, a horseshoe. A kind of U shape."

"Couldn't they ever look like a deer's track?"

Zeb ran a hand over the light, silky hair. Poor baby and her Pegasus dream, the one thing that Knobs would never find in this forest or any other. But she could not bring herself to crush the hope completely. "Possibly, but it's not too likely, precious. I'm satisfied that these are the tracks of a doe or a buck."

"Maybe there are fawns!" Fay spoke up. "Maybe not, though. When are they born?"

"Spring or early summer," Zeb said. "Yes, there could be, Fay. Let's believe it, shall we? Indeed, Squad, let's believe that this is only the beginning. The Belding squirrel. Unmistakable evidence of deer. Who knows?" She leaned her head back, gazing toward the hidden peaks above timber line. "Perhaps even mountain sheep with their beautiful, thick horns like cornucopias fastened to their brows. Being lost has its rewards." Feeling Knobs move apprehensively nearer, she added. "Not lost. Only a bit off the trail." She bent to the deer tracks again and spied a heap of droppings nearby. The droppings steamed in the moist air, proof that they were fresh.

"Squad," Zeb said softly, "our lovely quarry passed here not long ago. If we walk carefully, and keep our voices low, we might see it, or them."

Fay clapped her hands together in an excess of delight, then retreated under Sylvie's swift "Sh-h-h! You'll scare them away."

"I didn't think," Fay murmured, remorse-stricken.

Lester knelt by the tracks, his gaze seemingly locked on them, his eyes dream-dazed, soft dark hair falling over his forehead.

Zebrina felt a lifting joy; "as if a lark took flight within her breast" was the way she described such rare experiences. How beautiful it was to see that handsome boy kneeling there, he of the deep thoughts and sophisticated imaginings, looking with reverence at so simple a thing as a deer's hoofprint. Tears misted her vision further so that she was glad enough to have Knobs's moist, grubby hand clutching hers as they continued on the deer trail.

The muted cries of "There's another track!" came every

few minutes as they proceeded onward, together with whispered admonitions to be still.

"Other animals use deer trails," Zeb told them, "so you might watch for their tracks as well."

They had hiked another half hour when Patrick paused again. "The trail divides, Aunt Zeb. Which fork should we take, I wonder?" He pointed out the descending trail on the left, the ascending one on the right. "If we want to lose altitude, we should take the left fork, shouldn't we?"

Zebrina considered, plucking at a small white hair that grew out from her chin. "We can't be sure that it goes down consistently, Patrick. Or, even if it does, it could lead us into the maze of an impassable ravine. You could be right, but then again—" She squinted toward the upward trail, making out the vague outline of a rise behind the forest. And, at her feet, the deer tracks turned to the right. Instinct pulled her in that direction. "Let's take the upward path, dear, at least for a trial run. Once we reach the crest of the hill we should be able to see our way."

Patrick was glad enough to have the decision made for him. He felt increasingly bewildered as to direction and was inclined to fear they were traveling in a circle.

"Are we going to rest when we get there?" Fay appealed, pulling herself along at a slow gait and obviously limping.

"What's wrong?" Zeb inquired.

"It's my heel—I have a blister and it's getting raw." Apology glazed her eyes.

"That's a pity, dear one. Do you think you can make it to the top of the rise? Then I'll see what I can do."

"I guess so," Fay answered. "I'll try."

"All right. All together then, Squad. March."

Zebrina's own feet felt weary and bruised as the group slowly attained the summit, but her zeal increased as the trees thinned and she glimpsed to her right, below, an emerald-green lake. The lake's pear shape and the striking greenness stirred her memory. It looked much like Center Lake where James had once caught a huge brown trout— still mounted up in the attic with The Heads. If so, Crystal Crag lay due west.

Something fluttered over her head.

"A silver butterfly!" Sylvie cried.

"We're supposed to be quiet, on account of the deer," Fay scolded her.

"It was a moth," Lester said. "I saw it settle on a branch and its wings stayed horizontal."

Whatever it was, the insect vanished. The group was silent, searching the shadowy air. There was a rapid *rat-tat-tat* and then a sharp but fluid cry, and a glimpse of a feathered shape swooping from one tree to another.

Zebrina pressed one hand to her breast and closed her eyes, clutching the echo of the familiar cry of the flicker to her. She did not need to see the black crescent on his breast nor the red color under his wings to recognize an old friend.

"Who's he?" Knobs questioned. "What's he doin'?"

Zeb opened her eyes. "A red-shafted flicker, treasure." She heard the staccato of his beak again and could dimly make out his busy head where he clung to the trunk of a fir tree. "He's hunting for insects in the bark—which means they also exist."

"Do insects bite?"

"Some," Zeb admitted. "But it's mostly a minor nuisance. Let's hurry on now. Fay, are you all right?"

Fay nodded, but in spite of her attempt to present a brave appearance, there was self-pity in her expression.

They were nearing the summit when Lester called out in an undertone from the rear, "Wait—here's something." His tone bore an undercurrent of excitement exceeding any before. Zeb swung around to look toward him. He said nothing more but kept staring down at the ground.

Patrick loped past Zeb toward Lester and stood staring in turn, his jaw hanging.

"Well, speak up. What is it, boys?" she demanded, letting her own voice rise, but nobody dared to shush her. She approached and saw that the two looked stunned and shaken. Peering once again down her nose, cupping a hand over her eyes, she saw why. There, directly in the middle of the trail, was the unmistakable imprint of a man's shoe. Off to the side, less clear among crushed ferns, was another footprint.

Fay looked at the print and then at Zeb, nervously chewing at a finger nail. Sylvie took a backward step, as if the alien track were a threatening snake. Even Knobs needed no instruction as to what the footprint signified. She pressed close to Zeb's side.

"It means there's somebody else up here, don't it, Auntie Zeb?" she quavered. Fear blanched her face. "It's a man's footprint—it's Silver Daddy's!" Her voice ended in a scream. "Oh, it's Silver Daddy's. I know it! He's come to steal me away. He'll kill me! Hide me, Auntie Zeb—just get me away. Please! Please!"

Fay reached out. "Knobs, honey—"

Sylvie clenched her fists. "Knobs, you'll scare away the deer."

"Celeste!" Zeb said firmly. "Knobs! Stop it. Listen." She shook Knobs gently by the shoulders. "Silver Daddy is not here. Listen to Auntie Zeb. He is in jail. Whoever the man is, he is not Silver Daddy. He may be some gentle young man out exploring like us, looking for mammals or geologic specimens. Come now, love."

Knobs continued sobbing, cowering back against Zeb, looking fearfully about. "I want to go home—I just want to get out of here."

"We will, we will," Zeb assured her. "But remember, Celeste, I need your help. If you're going to cry and cringe like this, what will I ever do? I'm counting on you, do you understand? Now take my hand, dear, and lead on like the brave girl you are."

Knobs sniffled and stood poised in indecision, arms straight at her sides.

"Wipe your nose," Zeb ordered.

Mechanically, Knobs pulled her handkerchief from the breast pocket of her shirt and swiped at her nose.

"That's better. Let's forget all about this and go on. We may still find our deer, if we haven't frightened them away. We want to be quiet, remember, love?"

Knobs swallowed the last of her sobs and held out one hand.

Around her and Zeb, the others murmured excitedly about the discovery. Patrick looked somber and concerned. Lester looked perplexed and even sad.

"Even if he is only an explorer," Lester said, "it spoils things. I liked thinking that we were the only ones here, that perhaps we were the first humans to see wild animals for years."

"We mustn't be selfish, Lester," Zeb reproved him gently, even though she sympathized. Some of the tang of solitude and the excitement of discovery had been destroyed by the intruder's footprints. Intruder. That was a harsh and selfish description to apply to an unknown fellow human being. "And he may be of assistance in helping us find our way."

When they reached the summit and she paused, cupping each eye firmly as she scanned the high peaks now visible for miles around, she knew that they would not need the stranger. There was Crystal Crag soaring clearly over mile-long Lake Martha. And there, to the left, was Mirror Mountain, its solid obsidian dome glinting under fleeting cloud shadows. Straight ahead was Munson Butte, and a distance to the west was the familiar, entrancing sparkle of Horseneck Falls. Place names fascinated Zeb and as her straining gaze lingered on the spuming froth of the falls she decided that it was appropriately named, resembling as it did the flying mane of a swift, riderless horse. Inspired, she called Knobs's attention to it.

"I think that's your Pegasus, love, there in Horseneck Falls. Can't you just see his flying mane and the flash of silver wings?"

Knobs moved closer to her, ignoring the falls, her neck turning in the direction of some wind-twisted timber behind the group. All the other members of the Squad stood in rigid postures, staring in the same direction, voiceless.

Slowly, Zeb turned from the glory of the falls, hands still cupped around her eyes.

The man stood only some thirty feet away, looking down at them from his slightly higher elevation, his legs straddled, a heavy-caliber rifle held crosswise in front of him. The base of Zebrina's spine itched suddenly, a symptom that occurred only in moments of shock and a fear that even she could not deny. Cursing her vision, she strove to make out his features, having a long-time trust in her ability to judge a person's character by the lineaments of face and body. Aside from the man's stance—which seemed belligerent—she could make out only long, curly blond hair under a droop-brimmed hat, and a chopped-off beard.

Mechanically she moved closer. One could not carry on a conversation at thirty feet. Furthermore, it was essential that she appear completely calm and even unsurprised for the sake of the children.

"Don't come no closer, missus," the man said. He shifted his rifle.

"My dear sir," Zebrina replied, "we're not going to hurt you." She knew that her response must seem ludicrous, considering her age and ponderous weight and the man's obvious armed superiority. Only then did she remember her own small-caliber rifle sticking up over her knapsack. Still, it was certainly not within easy reach. No, it was not her gun he feared so much as the mere presence of other human beings, for reasons known only to him. Possibilities went rapidly through her mind. A prospector guarding some rare mineral discovery? A hermit jealous of his solitude? An escaped fugitive? The thought of Silver Daddy nudged her. No, she had seen newspaper photos of Silver Daddy, and this man, whatever else he was, was not the plump, dark-haired person who had played his evil role in Knobs's life.

"You don't need to cling to that gun so tightly, young man," she spoke out. "Mine is not even loaded. We are only a group of nature lovers, searching for wildlife. We wandered out of our way, and we certainly did not intend to disturb anyone." She gestured. "That is Crystal Crag over there, if I am not mistaken. What would you advise as to the shortest route down to what was once Highway 339?"

The children had moved up and stood slightly behind her in a silent row. After a moment, Patrick stepped ahead and stood erect, wide-eyed and pale-cheeked, directly beside her.

The man considered her and the rest of the Squad silently. His eyes seemed small and by their shifting glint she judged that he kept glancing warily from side to side. There was no doubt that he was highly nervous, and therefore dangerous.

"I'd go down that draw there," he said, releasing one hand from his rifle long enough to jab a thumb toward a reddish-brown cut that traversed the slope of a solidified lava flow. "Follow that about five miles and when you reach Harp Springs—there's some geysers there—you turn left. You can't miss."

"But—" Zeb began, then stopped her tongue. That would be in the wrong direction, she was positive. She felt Crystal Crag shining at her back, a beacon indicating the northeasterly direction that they must follow to reach the highway. Was he trying deliberately to mislead them, sending them deeper into the wilderness? If so, why? Again, her spine itched. She strained to inspect the man more closely, praying for a miracle that would restore her eyesight. There was no miracle, but even without it she could see that his clothes were ragged, his shoes frayed. From the corner of her vision she contemplated Patrick's large-sized, sturdy boots, and thought of the valuable gear they all carried, from food to medicines to sleeping bags. These would be treasure to the watchful and hostile stranger. Further, if he were truly an escaped convict, he would be concerned that they might alert the police.

"Above five miles down the draw?" she repeated, stalling for time. "And then left at the geysers. Is it a fairly clear trail?"

"Clear enough, if you keep your eyes open."

"I see. Thank you." She remembered Fay's blister, and her own aching feet. "If you don't mind, I think we'll rest first. We're a bit tuckered." She added with as much brightness as she could muster, "We saw deer tracks, unbelievably! In fact, we were hoping to see a deer or two up here."

"If you hadn't made so damned much noise, you might have," the man said, resentment close to sorrow in his voice.

So that was it, and that was why his boot print had been on the trail. He was stalking deer.

"I'm sorry," she said. "More than one deer?"

"Could be," he answered curtly.

She sat down, and the young people followed her cue.

She drank from her canteen and each of the Squad members, in turn, copied her.

Patrick cleared his throat and addressed the bearded sentry who stood watching them. "Uh—we didn't think there would be any deer up here at all. Not even birds."

"Yeah?"

Sylvie, not to be outdone by Patrick's boldness, asked, "Are you a hunter?"

The man said, "You're kind of a nosey kid, ain't you?"

Sylvie's eyelashes swept her cheeks, then she snapped her head up angrily. "We've as much right to be here as you have!"

"Sh-h-h," Fay whispered. "He might shoot us."

Zebrina considered. The man's nerves were obviously worn thin. He seemed young, perhaps barely twenty, and she felt some sympathy toward him for their having ruined his chance at the deer meat and hides that he evidently needed, at the same time that she was glad they had saved the deer. "The girl didn't mean to be impudent," she told him. Slyly, or so she hoped, she asked, "Are there any other animals around here?"

He did not answer immediately, and his mouth twitched. He hitched up his shoulders, pride evident in the gesture. "Yeah. A lot more than people down in the cities know!" The words rushed out then, and Zeb knew that he had not talked to another human being in a long while and was driven to brag about his prowess. "Bears, even. I shot me a fat brown bear two months ago that some of them old-time trophy hunters would have given their eyeteeth for. Mountain goat, too. I've got his horns on my shack. I—" He broke off, eyeing them closely again, fear and threat glistening in his eyes. "I'll give you ten minutes, and then you clear out, understand? The next time you interfere with my hunting, things will be different—and don't forget it."

He turned, put the rifle over his shoulder, and continued up the trail, alternately glancing back over his shoulder and studying the path for deer sign.

"Quick, love," Zeb told Fay. "Strip off your boot. Lester, the medicine kit." She took time to peer off toward the trees where the hunter had disappeared, or pretended to disappear. He would be there watching and waiting, she knew, the rifle at ready.

"It ain't Silver Daddy," Knobs whispered at her elbow.

"No dear, I told you that." She reached for the vial of antiseptic Lester held out to her, even as she spoke to Patrick. "Take your knife, dear, and cut out a hole in the heel of Fay's shoe, to spare the rubbing." She groped for the vial and, to her great disgust, found her hand shaking.

"How ridiculous," she said. "That's what happens when you nip wine against the doctor's orders. The shakes, my dears."

"You mean you're an alcoholic, Aunt Zeb?" Lester said with a wan grin.

"And let it be a warning to you," she replied, knowing that not one of them, even Knobs, was deceived. In spite of her obvious distress, she felt their eyes on her, trusting, relying on her.

"Patrick," she whispered, "do you know how to use a rifle?"

"No," Patrick confessed reluctantly. "But I could learn fast."

Lester hesitated, not remembering whether or not he had ever mentioned to Zeb his experience with guns. But her gaze had switched toward him. Perhaps he had foolishly bragged of his marksmanship. "I know how," he said, at last.

"Load it then, love. It carries a round of twenty shots." She saw the group's faces grow taut. "Not that we'll need it, but it's rather silly to carry it around unloaded, isn't it? I mean, a mother bear with cubs, if startled, might be troublesome—a warning shot in the air would probably take care of the matter. And, if our hunter can be believed, there are bears around."

Her face grimmer than she knew, Zebrina bandaged Fay's heel while her mind plunged ahead. They would take the trail the man had recommended, she decided, to deceive him, until they could safely head back in the right direction.

She observed Lester loading the .22, his lips drawn back in distaste. There would be no attacking bears, she believed, nor menacing mountain lions. The foe, if such he was, wore a drooping hat and faded dungarees.

She doubted that she could pull a trigger, even in self-defense. But in defense of the children . . . In any case, she was a poor shot, and her lack of glasses made the whole fantastic idea impossible.

"Lester," she said, "perhaps you should carry the rifle from now on."

He moistened his lips. "All right," he said, reluctance showing in every feature.

# CHAPTER 12

WE'D better hurry, Aunt Zeb," Patrick said, looking at
his watch and then toward the woods where the hunter
had disappeared.

"I refuse to be intimidated by that churlish young man,"
Zeb responded, although she was obviously hurrying as
much as possible, tearing open a packet of emergency
food. "Here," she said, thrusting Nutro-bars to the group.
"We may not have time for a proper meal. Lester, make
absolutely sure the rifle is on safety."

He held it up for her inspection.

"All right, then, Squad. If we're all ready—"

Patrick took his place at the head of the file. "Let's go."

Lester followed Fay at the rear. With the gun strapped
to his pack he felt as if he were the rear guard of an infantry
column invading foreign territory. Once through the short,
rocky draw, the path led down steeply into a creek-cooled
ravine, the banks dark-green with fern and water cress. To
the right of the path, the land sloped gradually upward,
woods and brush thinning out as the group progressed so
that he could make out an almost-treeless slope above. He
did not like the damp gloom of the ravine. It felt like a
trap rather than an escape route, even though he under-

stood the need to make the hunter believe they were following his instructions. Until they were far enough away
from the man to escape detection there was nothing to do
but proceed before correcting course, as Zeb had explained.

"Now we won't probably never see any deer," Knobs
mourned, her hand in Zeb's.

"Don't despair, sweet. We may see them and even other
wild creatures, if our bearded friend is to be believed."

Lester tried to shut out the sound of their voices, straining to catch what seemed to be a rustling noise in the
thicket some fifty feet above the path. He lagged back,
letting the others outdistance him, although he was careful to keep them in view. Apparently even keen-eared
Patrick had heard nothing. Lester strove to mute his footsteps and keep his eyes fixed ahead, for if the man were
up there, spying, it was safer to pretend ignorance of the
fact—unless the stranger was hunting not deer now, but
them.

Lester's jaws ached with tension, and he quickened his
pace. The rifle riding his back was the Squad's only protection. He drew the edge of his hand across his wet forehead, telling himself that he was letting apprehension
govern his good sense. Just because the man was rough-
looking and inarticulate didn't mean that he was a killer.
What purpose would his shooting them serve, except to
destroy witnesses against him? Even though almost everyone believed that game animals had disappeared long ago,
the game laws were still on the books and it was a felony
for anyone to hunt any prey except wild dogs. From Lester's experience, it would seem that very few of those
remained.

Again, he thought he heard the crack of a twig under a moving weight, and permitted himself to glance toward the sound. It seemed to have come from the very edge of the timber on his upper right, at a forward angle where the trees thinned and the land sloped down toward an open meadow. Patrick was swinging ahead, setting a faster pace as the group prepared to cross the open stretch at the meadow's edge, and Lester increased his own stride. The stiffness of Patrick's back, and his speed, told Lester that perhaps Patrick had not been deaf to the underbrush cracklings and was intent on leading the Squad as swiftly as possible toward the other side of the meadow where again the path plunged into high-walled, protective gloom.

He heard Fay panting in an effort to keep up the brisk pace and saw that though she limped less, she favored the bandaged foot. In his haste and concentration on the upper woods, he almost trod on her heels. "Sorry," he whispered, and then repeated the word aloud to remove the aura of fear the whisper created.

If the man really was lurking there, the rifle aimed, what then? Nervously, Lester pushed his hair out of his eyes. He had vowed to himself, staking all his integrity and his belief in nonviolence on the vow, that he would never intentionally injure another creature, including his fellow man. He should not have let Aunt Zeb entrust him with the gun. He hated himself. First the blunder with the compass, and now this. He had to restrain himself from rushing past Fay and Sylvie and thrusting the rifle back into Zeb's hands, or even into Patrick's. Patrick had never handled a gun but Pat knew what a trigger was and he would not hesitate to squeeze it if necessary.

No, that was only a way of escaping responsibility and pushing the burden on somebody else.

But I can't shoot anyone, Lester thought, torn by the irony of his natural talent for marksmanship and all the knowledge of weapons forced on him by his father. Briefly, a picture of his father rose before him, splendid in his Space Marine uniform, chest emblazoned with ribbons. "You've got an eye for the target, son. All you need is the will."

The picture vanished, replaced by a startling tableau. Patrick had stopped and was staring directly down the meadow. In a motionless row stood Zeb, Knobs, Sylvie, and now, directly ahead of Lester, Fay.

Lester glanced wildly up the slope, certain that the others had spotted the hunter. For he was there. Lester saw him crouched in the shadows of thickly growing Sierra snow-bush covered with masses of white flowers. The blossoms' fragrance wafted toward Lester, and he saw the glint of the man's gun. But it was not pointing at the Squad.

Lester's gaze swung back to the meadow even as he hurried ahead to alert Zeb. He brushed past Fay and Sylvie.

"Zeb," he appealed in a hoarse whisper. "He's up there —he's—"

"Sh-h-h," she said, cautiously lifting one pointing finger.

He saw the three mule deer, a doe and twin fawns, dark tails flickering to reveal a glimpse of the white underside. The trio was partially concealed by the swatches of bitter brush on which they were feeding. There was no time for him to enjoy their beauty in the rush of horror that swept over him, for now he knew why the hunter was poised above, his rifle in direct line with the animals.

The doe began to move out warily from her shelter, sniffing the air.

"Zeb!" He clutched her elbow. "He's up there—on the hill, drawing a bead on them!"

"Wh-what?" Zeb stammered. She cast a distraught glance toward the hill, then toward the meadow, her eyes shifting in confusion, her mouth agape.

"Don't you understand—he's up there, ready to shoot!"

Comprehension spread across Zebrina's features. She moved with such swiftness, in spite of her weight and aging bones, it was as if her muscles for a lifetime had been tensed and ready for this moment. The hiking skirt waved out behind her wide hips; the light helmet went sailing off her head with the wind of her speed, the meadow grass crushed by the urgency of her feet. Directly opposite the deer, who now stood with heads up, the fawns stepping back daintily behind the doe, the glossy eyes of all startled and alert, Zebrina stopped.

In the center of the mountain-circled scene, exposed to the sky and the broad space of the meadow, Zeb paused. Like a traffic policeman of earlier times at a busy intersection, she lifted her right hand, palm spread out, facing the invisible gunman on the hill. "Stop!" she shouted. "You shall not shoot. I forbid it!"

It was like a still shot from a movie, Lester thought, staring at Zeb in concern and admiration. Fearless, her white hair lifted by a breeze from the thin lips of the ravine, she remained with her hand imperiously upraised. Behind her, the doe stood motionless, head reared. A fraction of a second before the shot, the doe wheeled and with a glorious

leap disappeared into the bitter brush, the fawns bounding
beside her.

Lester let his breath out in relief. The hunter had missed.
He felt his muscles sag, his fear ebb, and then Patrick—or
perhaps it was Sylvie—yelled, "Les, the gun! Get it!"

He fumbled at it mechanically, stripping it from its
rack, thumb automatically releasing the safety catch as he
saw the hunter plunge down from his hiding spot. The
heavy rifle was cradled against the hunter's shoulder.

"You old bag!" the man shouted at Zebrina. "Get outta
here! I could have shot your fool head off. I should have.
It's not too late!" He slowed but approached her at a steady
gait, the muzzle aimed directly at her chest. "I'll teach you
to come bumbling around here where you're not wanted—
you and those yapping kids, getting between me and my
game, twice. I warned you—" He stopped, only five yards
away, and leaned his cheek against the gunstock, his finger
tight on the trigger.

Knobs screamed, started toward Zeb, then retreated to
Fay's sheltering arms. "Don't look!" Fay cried, bringing
her palm up over Knobs's eyes, turning her own face away
from the angry man.

Lester shouted toward the bearded hunter, his voice
breaking, his eye fixed to the sight of the .22. "Drop your
gun or I'll—"

The man spun toward him, the muzzle aimed straight at
Lester.

"You spindly son-of-a—" the man snarled.

Lester took careful aim, feeling that his arms and legs
and scalp were enclosed in ice, and squeezed the trigger.

The hunter's rifle cracked almost simultaneously so that it seemed an echo of the .22.

The blast of the two guns tore a double, jagged hole in the silence, followed by the harsh, unexpected notes of a crow.

Lester stared at the figure of the hunter spilling to the earth, the rifle skittering from his grasp, both hands grabbing at his left leg. Though transfixed by horror and dismay, Lester heard the raucous dark cry above, and marveled. The crow's shadow swept across the meadow. Lester, still clutching his own weapon, went racing toward Zeb.

"You did what you had to do, darling," she said, seeing the look on his face. With that, she hurried toward the stranger. Patrick, following, raced to the man's rifle and picked it up.

"Watch it, mister," Patrick commanded from his sudden position of power. He clutched the gun as if it were something that could leap from his grasp, his hands and whole manner awkward, but his eyes triumphant.

The young man lay back on one elbow, both hands clutching his bloody ankle, glaring at Zeb, his deep-green eyes still defiant in spite of his grimace of pain. "Don't come near me. Get outta here, like I said." He wrenched his neck around, looking toward Crystal Crag, which showed its gray thumb above the meadow. "My buddy'll be along in a minute. He'll take care of all of you."

Zebrina paused only a few feet away, compassion creasing her face. "Don't be silly," she said. "We have to stop the bleeding. Just look at you. Much more of that"—she gestured toward the red pool forming around his foot— "and it won't matter when your buddy shows up. And he won't, because you don't have one. No man that I would call a man would be a partner of a person who would slaughter a mother deer in cold blood and leave two helpless babies to a slow, miserable death. You can't lie to me, young man. Now, let's remove your shoe and sock. Lester, the medical kit. Lester!"

He had slumped down in the cool grass, his head swimming from the sight of the blood—blood that he had caused to flow; he, the follower of St. Francis, Gandhi, Schweitzer. Sickness swirled in his stomach, and all sounds and sights blurred.

"Hey, Les," Patrick prompted, bending over him. "That was a slick shot, pal." He held the hunter's rifle awkwardly.

Lester could not answer. He mustered the strength to reach up and fasten the safety lock on the rifle. "Be—careful, Pat." He dipped his face into his cupped hands again.

"Aunt Zeb says to get the med kit," Sylvie spoke close to his ear. "You were wonderful, Lester."

He shrugged out of his pack. "Right here—top flap."

He permitted himself to look toward the spot where the man lay, seeing how Zeb was kneeling beside him, her hands broad and heavy-knuckled against the man's wound. The lower part of his leg and foot were bare, wan against the greens and browns of the turf.

"Lie still!" she commanded the still-growling and protesting stranger. "If you won't co-operate, I can't be responsible for what happens."

"I don't need nobody taking care of me," he said. "Never had anybody doing it before. I can take care of myself, see?"

"And what you can't take care of, the vultures will finish," Zeb said. "If there are any."

The man eyed her. "Shows how much you know. Lots of 'em. You should have seen the bones of a fox they cleaned up last week."

"A fox," Zeb breathed. "Where?" She removed the compress and peered down at the bullet wound.

"I don't have to say," he answered and tried to stifle a groan as she probed the wound.

"You won't be hiking anywhere—or hunting helpless deer—for a long while, young man." She swabbed the wound, then began wrapping gauze around the foot, ankle, and leg. "Awfully dirty toenails, I must say." He was hunched back, supported uncomfortably on his elbows. "Fay, bring one of the bedrolls for a pillow."

"You don't have to fuss about me," the young man said, but a vague wonder had replaced the anger in his eyes. "What're you folks doing out here, anyhow?"

"I told you. Looking for surviving wildlife and plants."

"Hah, rich people like you don't go traipsing around wilds like these for that kind of stuff."

Zeb stood up, her hands stained red, her face flushed from her exertions. She looked down at him calmly as Fay daringly pushed a bedroll under his blond, shaggy head. "You are a very ignorant, suspicious, and hostile person, and the sooner you gain some education and civility, the better. Now, be quiet while I clean myself up and arrange some proper food for my young friends and myself. You've given us far more than enough trouble for one day."

She turned to the group, briskly slapping her palms

together. "What we need is a fire for cooking, some water, and a good rest."

Passing Lester, she paused. He felt her hand on his shoulder, firm and yet gentle. "The world is what it is, dear, and not another thing." She marched on, barking her commands to the Squad like a platoon leader.

The world is what it is. He supposed so. Who didn't know that? It seemed a very simplistic observation for Zebrina to make. But when he faced the statement clearly, he realized that he, as long as he could remember, had been dedicated to changing the world. He held his long fingers outstretched, working them, wrenching at the invisible and imperfect fabric of the world and man. Surely it was essential to try to change things, wasn't it? But change, too, was a fact. The fact was what *was*. And the fact was that he had deliberately maimed a human brother.

Brother? He looked toward the supine, bearded figure, leg bandaged below the rolled-up portion of his faded trouser leg, and recalled the epithet the man had hurled at him. Had the hunter really been tracking them, or had his pursuit of the deer only coincidentally brought him to the meadow at the same time the Squad arrived there? After all, the rifle had been aimed first at the doe, only switching to Zeb and then himself at the last moment.

Brother Fire, Brother Ass, Brother Louse. The ghost of St. Francis seemed to walk barefooted across the meadow. St. Francis had never shot anyone. Lester studied his own well-shod feet, arose, and walked toward the stranger.

"I was wondering," he said, head lowered, feeling embarrassment, "do you need water or anything?" He touched the canteen at his side.

The stranger looked at him and raised his head weakly from his improvised pillow, silent.

"I mean, I'm sorry— I thought you were going to shoot her. Or me."

"You reckoned right, Spindly."

The sneer was unmistakable and Lester winced. "My name is Lester," he said with strained dignity.

"You don't say!"

He felt anger surge through him and knew that he should turn away, but he remained, meeting the other's contemptuous gaze. "Young man," Zeb had called the stranger. He was certainly twenty or more. Space Cadets were manning space stations at age eighteen. Lester would become one of them, if his father had his way.

"The name is Lester," he repeated. "Lester Paullin. And, as I said, I'm sorry."

"That makes everything O.K., don't it?" The man propped himself up on his elbow at the cost of a groan. "Well, my name's Joshua—right out of the Bible—so how do you like that, you spindly, snaky, sniggering sneak?" The green eyes held a wild, accusing gleam. "Nature lover, huh? I'd like to see you live off the land! Maybe you can shoot pretty good, or else you were just lucky. Whatever, don't come sniveling around afterward wanting me to pat you on the head and say 'It's all right, sonny boy.' "

Lester's cheeks burned. He choked back the hot words that rose to his own lips, and turned. As he hurried away he visualized the man spitting at his back.

Fay looked up as he approached the campsite. "If it hadn't been for your quick action, I don't know what would have happened to save—"

"Shut up!" he cried, the boil of hurt and anger bursting in him, and then, as fierce-eyed as the wounded Joshua, he fled blindly across the meadow toward some place where he could be alone, beyond the sound of any voice.

He found a retreat among a stand of young pines and sat there brooding, striving to recapture the mood he had been in when he had thought of St. Francis. Perhaps he had deserved the wounded man's sneers. For hadn't he really gone to him in the hope that Joshua would forgive him and thereby alleviate his feeling of guilt? Certainly it had been cruel of him to lash out at Fay like that, and he must apologize.

He was still deep in introspection some ten minutes later when he saw the buck move into a clearing only twenty feet away. The animal paused, its antlers like a many-branched candelabrum on its head, its eyes dark and glowing. Lester sucked in his breath at the beauty of the creature, feeling that he and it were one and the same, being only separate forms of the life stuff that permeated the universe. He recalled Aunt Zeb standing like a statue of the law, her stout body interposed between the hunter and the doe, her broad hand upraised. The buck looked directly at Lester, then calmly dipped its head to nibble green shoots from a nearby bush before it walked slowly beyond his sight.

As Lester got to his feet, he felt empty of all sensation except a grateful humility, for the moment had been a special gift. From whose hand he did not know, nor did he want to destroy the beauty of the vision by wondering. The world is what it is.

He walked back to the smoking campfire, eager to resume the companionship of the Squad and ready to share in the activity. "What can I do to help?" he asked.

"There are three live spuds left," Sylvie said with a grin. "Somebody ought to peel them."

"Heroes don't peel potatoes," Patrick said.

"Enough of that," Zebrina said and looked toward the slope where their erstwhile enemy lay. "What, Squad, are we going to do about that poor creature?"

Nobody answered. A shadow floated across the meadow and trees. Zeb looked up. A turkey vulture, as the hunter had said. The circling wings were dim to Zeb's sight, the naked head invisible, but the soaring shape was unmistakable. It was enough, or almost enough, she thought, to replace the long-vanished California condor.

"One gift after another!" Zeb exclaimed, and Lester was struck by her expressing exactly what he had felt a few moments before. She placed a fresh piece of wood on the fire and continued where she had left off. "We can't leave him lying there alone, of course."

Again there was silence, broken only by the crackle of the fire and a rustling in the meadow brush. The rustling could have been the doe and the fawns, or a chipmunk, or even a brown bear. One thing it was not was Josh Miller, lying in frustration, pain, and fear on his bloodied slope of wilderness.

# CHAPTER 13

JOSH Miller refused the food Zebrina offered him, looking at the aluminum plate in disdain. "Just give me back my gun and I'll manage to crawl to my own place and fix myself some grub." He was in an upright position now, and for all his braggadocio he was obviously in pain, the wounded ankle swollen under the bandages. "You got no right to steal my gun off me."

"Where is your place?"

"You're the last person I'd ever tell, missus. Bring me my rifle over here and clear out, unless you want real trouble."

"You may have a Biblical name, Joshua," she said, having learned this from Lester, "but that's the end of any resemblance. More important, you are not even using your head. The only way you can reach your house, or cave, or whatever it is, is with our help. And even then it won't be easy."

"I'd reach it all right. I can fix myself up a crutch when I get there. Don't you worry about me."

"How far away is it?"

"Not so far."

"It certainly isn't visible from here."

"Lots of things exist that ain't visible."

"That's true," Zeb admitted, thinking that perhaps Josh was not so stupid as he appeared. But his stubbornness was stupid, and one of the things that most affronted her nature was to have food rejected. She pushed the plate at him. "Take this and eat it before it's completely cold. You'll need your strength, young man, to crawl back to your hut. We have little enough to spare, let alone waste on an ungrateful mouth."

Still he looked with disdain at the plate, though she detected a glimmer of longing over the portion of boiled potato. It was unlikely, she thought, that he was able to raise any garden things where he was, so he probably existed almost exclusively on venison or whatever he could trap, with perhaps some edible wild plants on the side.

"Well, eat it or not," she snapped, setting the plate and utensils down within his reach. "I don't have time to stand here bickering. We shall be on our way within one half hour, and then you will be alone, as you seem to long to be. I only trust that your shelter is not far, as you claim, that you have medicines and clean bandages available, and that there are no complications such as blood poisoning."

On that deliberately alarming note, she walked back toward the meadow's edge and the fire which Sylvie was damping in its ashes. Zeb's own food had grown cold in the interval. She was too troubled to care, and spooned the meal into her mouth mechanically, trying to reach a decision. It seemed to her that the Squad could now cut back from the meadow, using Crystal Crag as a landmark. With any luck, they could manage it in two days, with one night's rest. There was more than enough dehydrated and concentrated food. Nor was water apt to be a problem, not at this elevation with springs, lakes, and creeks.

"What are you going to do about *him*, Aunt Zeb?" Fay ventured, eyeing the distant Josh.

Zeb sighed and reached absently toward the bridge of her nose to adjust her nonexistent glasses. "The only way we could take him with us would be on a stretcher."

Patrick, standing alongside, thumbs hooked into his belt, declared, "He's pretty skinny. I could tote him on my back. Or Les and I could support him between us."

"Perhaps." Zeb's tone was doubtful. "I don't question your strength, dear, but the difficulties of the trail. We could strive to take him to his shack, if he would co-operate, and try to make him comfortable there; then, when we reach home, try to enlist the Rescue Force to fly in and find him. It's difficult to think of leaving him where he is, without food or shelter." She contemplated her bedroll, wondering if she could sacrifice it to the deer killer. A vision of herself after a chill night, or perhaps two or three, aching with rheumatism or wheezing with pneumonia, a half-blind and sick burden on the youngsters, pushed the consideration from her mind. She could perhaps spare her canteen for him. What foolish speculations! It was impossible to leave him in any case.

Was there the barest chance, she wondered, that there were other persons in the area who might hear her rifle if she fired a series of distress signals? She discounted Josh's reference to a "buddy," but possibly there might be some explorer or prospector or even scouts from the military base. It could be worth a try.

The sun was past its zenith now. Indecision could not continue. She stood up heavily. "I'll go talk with him again and see if I can persuade him to guide us to wherever he stays, until we can arrange for help. Without medical attention, anything could happen."

The shadows of the tall trees edging the meadow fell over her as she turned and peered toward the indistinct image of Josh Miller. She reached out her hand for Knobs, whose help she had eschewed earlier.

"He won't hurt you, love," she prompted as Knobs held back. "What's the matter?"

Then she heard the distant drone, swiftly changing to a shrill, throbbing whine, though she could not make out the shark-nosed objects swooping down past an enormous thunderhead.

"Super-sentries!" Patrick yelled. "Five of them. They don't see us!"

"Flatten out!" Sylvie cried, throwing herself face down against the earth.

Zeb had a blurred vision of Fay racing toward the protection of the trees. "No, Fay! If they topple—"

Her cry was cut short as the fleet of sleek, whistling military planes, practicing their maneuvers, slanted down toward the meadow. Pulling Knobs with her, Zeb crashed against the ground, her arm crooked protectively about the little girl. Except for the *whoosh* of metal wings slicing the air, everything was ominously silent for an instant. Then she felt the blast of the streaming engines, so powerful that it rolled her over and pulled Knobs from her grasp. Her hair whipped across her eyes; she struggled to her knees, groping for the child. The earth shook and a

thunderous *boom* pounded her eardrums. A branch hurtled
through the air and struck her temple, while all around,
as if sucked by an enormous pump, strips of turf rolled
and tumbled like prehistoric serpents. Pebbles and even
rocks, flung up from the creek, crashed around the area,
striking her back and shoulders.

Curse them, curse them, she thought, her arms sheltering her head. They were not supposed to be here. The
Lost Lakes region was off limits to military maneuvers,
as New City was supposed to have been when the SST had
cracked the dome.

The boom had passed, but still branches, clumps of
uptorn turf and stones rained down, while the border of
trees creaked in their sockets, several grinding to earth.
Then it was over and Zeb dared to raise her head, searching
for her charges, rising unsteadily to her feet. Unaware of
blood trickling down from her left temple, she stared about
in confusion and grim dismay. Almost everything they had
lugged with them—sleeping bags, canteens, food kits—
was gone. Even the embers of the fire that they had been
about to extinguish had been swept away. She pressed a
hand to her forehead, swaying, seeing an image of the
embers flying across the jet-created wind like a swarm of
fireflies.

"Auntie Zeb!" Knobs's weak voice called. Zeb squinted,
cupped her hands around her eyes, and followed the voice.
"I'm on my way, treasure—I'll be right there." She found
Knobs half-buried by a swatch of uprooted slough grass
and pulled her free. Swiftly she ran exploring hands over
her, searching for wounds or broken bones.

"I ain't hurt," Knobs said shakily. "But you are, Auntie

—oh, there's blood runnin' down!" She took a step in one
direction, then the other. "I'll get help. I'll get the medicine kit—" She stopped, mouth sagging open. "It ain't
here. Nothin's left!" She spied Lester, who was resting on
one knee, looking blankly at the sky, and ran toward him.
"Zeb's hurt—get the medicine!"

Zebrina drew a shuddering breath. "Fay!" she called
toward the forest. "Fay!"

Patrick, apparently unscathed, loped toward Zeb. "She
ran into the woods—and then the trees started falling."
He wheeled toward the timber, then shouted, "There she
is!"

Fay appeared under her own power, but Patrick hurried
toward her and put a solicitous hand under her elbow.

"That was stupid, to run into the woods," he said.
"That's one of the worst places."

Her teeth were chattering. "Well, it was stupid for the
Sentries to swoop over like that, too."

Lester came forward, followed by Sylvie, both dirt-
streaked and disheveled. Sylvie's once-crisp outfit was
torn. She fussed with it in a distraught way, her eyes still
glassy with shock.

Lester gripped his left wrist with his right hand.
"Sprained it, I guess, when I got knocked off my feet."

"Is everyone all right?" Zebrina asked at least three
times, weaving from one to the other, inspecting, com-
miserating.

"We seem to be alive, luckily," Patrick said. "Some
wilderness! I wonder if the animals ever get killed."

Zeb fumbled at the cloth band around her helmet,
which she had miraculously retrieved, unfastened it,

mopped at her bloody face, then wrapped the band tightly around her forehead. Her head aching fiercely, she surveyed her small, unkempt band. None except Knobs had seemed to notice their vanished goods—or presumably vanished, if she could trust her eyesight.

"Yes, we are alive, Squad," she said, trying to assume some composure and confidence. "But things may have become a bit more difficult since our Air Force defenders blundered into our lost Eden. It would seem that most of our supplies have been blown to kingdom come. Our first job is to search for and try to recover whatever is within a reasonable distance. But stay within the sound of each other's voices, and be prepared to return when I blow my whistle."

"Shall I go, too?" Knobs asked.

"No, love. I'll need you here."

Authoritatively, Patrick took over. "Les, you and Sylvie go together as a unit. Take the creek side. Fay and I will search the meadow and the woods."

They started off, and it was only then that Zeb remembered Joshua Miller. "Poor young man," she said. "Knobs, we'd better go see about him."

He sat as he had been before, the bedroll still supporting the small of his back. Even the plate remained where Zeb had placed it, but its contents had been eaten. The weeds and grass around Josh were undisturbed, the destructive swath having stopped short of him.

At least one bedroll had been saved, Zeb thought, for what it was worth.

Josh scarcely noticed her or Knobs. He was staring at the thunderhead and the blue sky around it, his right fist clenched. "That's what I came here to get away from! They were always there, right at the edge of my town; they didn't come over, but you could hear them all the time. You couldn't keep a horse there—it drove the horses crazy. Even the dogs and cats left, and all the birds. Then the people left, too, including me. Only most went to the cities, but that was worse. I tried that, too. But I always wanted a horse—only you can't keep a horse out here, either. I mean, they die, eating the wrong things, or they run off and join a wild herd. I spent a hundred bucketfuls of sweat getting one up here, and then—" He shook his head. "The only safe place for horses is in the cities where they got stables and bridle paths. And race tracks. You talk about meanness to animals!"

"You ate your food, I notice," Zeb cut in.

Josh shrugged. "After the Sentries swooped over, why not? It's a wonder they left anything standing, including you. Not that you look so high and mighty now, with that bloody rag."

She sat down almost casually beside him, and Knobs crawled into her lap. "I am not high and mighty and have never wanted to be, Joshua. Indeed, it would seem that we are all in trouble. If you truly have a house of refuge that could accommodate yourself and six guests, with a modicum of water and food, perhaps we could work out some arrangement."

"So now you're on the begging end."

"No, I daresay the Squad could push through. I'm only suggesting a mutual accommodation. We'll help you to your place, do what we can for you, and then—"

"And then call in the Patrol."

"What have you done that you're so afraid of?" she asked. "Have you killed someone?"

He ran his tongue around his teeth. "Sure. Deer, one mountain goat—and his meat was mighty tough—maybe a dozen pigeons, and one brown bear. A man's got to eat and have a blanket on winter nights."

"I eat, and keep warm, without having to kill wild creatures."

"Oh, sure," he said. "I know. You're huddled under a dome somewhere, and all your meat's killed in an underground, fluorescent-lighted lab, so you never have to get your hands bloody. Ain't that the truth?"

"I'm not a vegetarian, if that's what you mean," she said. "That's another question. But there's no threat to the bovine species, or sheep, or kine, nor to horses, for that matter. It's a different matter with deer, mountain goats, and bear, or birds. Why should you destroy their hope of survival for your own romantic idea of independence? That's all it is, young man. And you are not independent now. Look at that leg!"

He gazed at it morosely. "It's somewhat bigger than it ought to be," he admitted.

"Try to stand on it—or even to crawl. The last I heard, you were going to crawl to your shelter."

"You think I can't stand?" he countered. He put his right hand on one knee, knuckles standing out, spine rigid, and somehow pulled himself to his feet. He was upright, though barely so, perspiration studding his face and beading his yellow beard. "There!" he exclaimed before he trembled, swaying, his eyelids clamping down over his eyes. Blood seeped from under the bandages. He staggered and slumped down, panting. "It don't mean I can't still crawl," he insisted, but there was defeat in his voice.

She shrilled on her whistle, looking toward the campsite. "When the children return, we'll work out some way to help you to your dwelling. In the meantime, rest and be sensible." She gave him a sidelong glance. "You didn't really intend to kill that beautiful doe, did you?"

"I sure did, old lady. And the fawns, too—you didn't have to worry about them being orphans."

"And me?"

"Maybe." He avoided her eyes. "One thing I forgot to mention. Crystal Lodge, where I hang out, is supposed to be loaded with contaminants."

*Supposed* to be. The words stuck in Zeb's mind. Steve, too, had been dubious of areas beyond the Lost Lakes region. She recalled the heavily shaded areas on her map, a map that had been issued at least ten years before. It was true that the Crystal Lake area was suspect. She had not aimed toward that, wanting only a glimpse of the huge crag to help them find their way. Now, obviously, they had blundered close to the crag, in spite of her earlier studies of the route.

"You look healthy enough," she said, "except for your leg. How long have you been in this area?"

"Long enough to be dead several times over, if the government experts are right."

She studied him and pondered. He had earlier said "months" in reference to his time spent here, so it had been no short-term residence. There had been the scorn of superior, first-hand knowledge when he mentioned the "government experts."

"I think we'll take the risk," she said.

He sank back, his head against the bedroll, seemingly indifferent now to her or to the figures of the Squad toiling up the incline.

Lester carried a sodden sleeping bag, a dented canteen, and the container holding Zeb's test meters. Patrick held the .22 rifle in the crook of one arm, a Foreverflash in his hand. Sylvie had a pack frame complete with bedroll on her back and, with it, the least essential item of all, the butterfly net. Fay appeared empty-handed until she came nearer and Zeb was able to make out the medical kit.

Patrick, red-faced from exertion, stood in front of Zeb. "We thought we saw the main food kit but it was way down at the bottom of the ravine. I don't know whether we could have recovered it, even if we'd tried."

"You did very well, Squad," Zeb said, and asked Fay to hand her the medical kit. She fumbled to open it, in search of gauze to swab at the blood still trickling from her forehead wound. She could judge by the children's expressions that she was a rather grisly sight, but there was no way to remedy that immediately. "What we are going to do now, dears, is to proceed to Mr. Joshua Miller's refuge, and there take a fresh look at the overall situation. As ancient Japanese painters used to put their heads between their legs to get a fresh view of the landscape by looking at it upside down, so we too will seek a new perspective. There is no need to panic, as I know you won't. I think it would be wise to sleep on the matter and make any final decisions in the morning." She looked toward Josh, then at Patrick. "A fireman's carry should do it, if you can manage."

"Which way?" Patrick asked.

Josh opened his eyes. He looked silently at Patrick, Zebrina, and the others, some reluctance still obvious in his expression, then inclined his head slightly toward the crest of the wooded hill. "That way," he murmured, his eyelids sagging.

He put up no resistance when Patrick stooped down and slung him over his back.

"I'll help when you get tired, Pat," Lester said, but he still gripped his left wrist, his mouth taut. He let go, bent down, and retrieved the .22 Patrick had laid down. Josh's rifle had disappeared along with all the other articles.

Zeb gave Lester's swollen wrist a studious glance, shook her head, and concentrated on dividing the few burdens evenly among the group. Already Patrick was striding upward in the direction Josh had indicated.

"How far, Josh?" she called out. "Can you please tell us how far?"

He opened his eyes briefly. " 'Bout a mile, straight west."

A mile! In steep terrain. Patrick would have to pause for frequent rests. It would be a grueling journey.

Zeb felt Knobs's hand groping for hers. "Thank you, sweet." She drew her other hand across her eyes as though to wipe away the slight giddiness that threatened her. "All right, Squad. On the march."

She was in the lead again, excepting Patrick lugging his burden steadily up the incline. What would they do once they reached Josh Miller's hideaway? She put the question aside. The vital thing now was to reach there.

Something skittered over the ground, almost across the tips of her stout shoes. She glimpsed a striped body, bright eye arrowed by dark fur.

"A chipmunk, loves!" she called out cheerfully. "Remember it." She trudged on in Patrick's slow wake. Who could tell when they would ever again see a chipmunk, or a doe and fawns, or even a crow, after this journey was over?

She looked up at the sky. It was empty, even the giant thunderhead having disappeared. Best of all, there were no more hurtling airplanes off limits. She thought of the young pilots buckled into their intricate machines, the complexities of space, the extreme velocities they had to cope with. She had cursed them in her panic. No, not them, but the complex forces they were supposed to be able to control.

Nearby, the skeleton of an abandoned mine-shaft head stood against the sky, starkly visible, the land around it gutted and eroded. She remembered her grandfather, trapped underground, a miner dying at his black trade. Man had never been able to control machines and advancing technology completely. Nor himself, most of all. Resolutely she put one aching foot ahead of the other. Such old thoughts, she reflected. Seeing a drop of blood splash from her temple onto the undergrowth, she added: and such old blood.

She stopped, needing to rest.

"Are you going to be all right, Auntie Zeb?" Knobs appealed, looking up at her with a return of hollow fear.

"Why, of course, sweet. I'm only a bit winded." They

would all be all right. No doubt of it. Pressed a little beyond expectation, true. But there was no real peril. And there was Patrick, the valiant, sweating his way upward with that animal killer on his back.

She could not hate the bearded young man. He was confused, desperate, for reasons of his own. As it was, he had accidentally provided them with a refuge, such as it might be. She strove to imagine the place as she drew herself up, tightened her grip on Knobs's hand, and went on.

# CHAPTER 14

THE sun still cleared the snow-touched peaks of the highest mountains when the climbers reached their destination. For the last tenth of a mile, Patrick and Lester had carried Josh together, making a hammock of their joined hands while Josh clung to the shoulders of both. Now, as Zebrina rounded a final turn in the trail, she saw the structures ahead. It was no shack that she was seeing, but a spacious building with many smaller units to one side. Built of peeled Douglas-fir logs, with a sturdy aluminum roof, the main lodge had withstood storm and abandonment so well that it looked as if at any moment tennis players might trot out toward the empty court, or swimmers race to the edge of the waterless pool. Across the ornately carved wood of the front door, wrought-iron letters proclaimed: *CRYSTAL LODGE*.

"Oh, it's beautiful," Fay said, thinking that it was far finer than the dilapidated frame house where she and her family lived in Old City.

Looking at the stalwart trees, the healthy grass and weeds, the brilliant sky, Zebrina thought that surely so beautiful a spot could not be contaminated. Josh's warning, she suspected, was meant to deter her from seeking out his hideaway. Nevertheless, she ordered the group to wait while she busied herself with her various meters and gauges, testing soil, air, and the water of a nearby brook.

"It's all right, dears," she said at last, and waved them on.

"Do we go in the front door?" Patrick asked Josh, looking toward the main lodge. Sweat dripped from his chin, and he looked haggard from his grueling climb.

Josh shook his head. "I got my quarters in one of the cabins at the side. The one with the fish pole leaning by the door. Lodge is too cold and empty. Gives a man the shivers."

Zeb and the others followed as the boys carried Josh the rest of the way. Sylvie pushed the unlocked door open.

The motel unit had been of the deluxe type, Zeb observed, following at the boys' heels. She bumped against the corner of a single bed near the door. "Lay him on that," she instructed, peering through the dim light within. The long room was crowded with a surfeit of furnishings, borrowings from the lodge or other units, and yet it was surprisingly neat. Old, faded comic books were stacked in an orderly row on a shelf next to an equally orderly row of boxes carrying photographs of bullets on their covers. A comfortable-looking overstuffed chair stood in one corner and Zeb yearned to sit in it. In another corner stood an oak drop-leaf table, unwashed dishes still on it, and a thick candle whose wax had dripped on to the bare wood. Zeb, who was fond of fine furniture, mourned at the sight. She tried to avoid seeing the bear rug beside the bed, or the deer antlers from which hung several articles of clothing.

Fighting fatigue, and with a lingering look again at the chair, she moved to the bed. Blood from Josh's wound was staining the already-soiled spread.

"Sylvie, see if there are any towels or linens in the bathroom." To Josh she said, "Where can we find water?"

"Tank just around the side. I keep it filled with spring water. Pure stuff."

"I'll want to boil it, nevertheless, for your wound." She peered around again. There had been no provision for cooking in the unit, and even if there had been there was no gas or electricity available. "Where do you cook, Josh?"

He lay with his eyes closed so long it seemed he either had not heard or was unable to answer. "Smokehouse—next door."

Knobs leading the way, Zeb investigated the adjacent unit. A crude tin chimney, evidently Josh's handiwork, ran up through a hole cut into the roof, with yet another opening at the other side. Entering, she saw a stove constructed from a fuel drum, a pile of wood beside it. Beyond, under a circular hole that admitted the blue sky, a shape hung from a horizontal beam. It resembled a sinewy, dark-brown piece of driftwood more than the smoked haunch of a deer.

"What's that?" Knobs asked.

"Just cured meat, love."

"Do people ever eat horses?"

"No, Celeste. Now, let's get busy and start a fire." Groping at a rough cupboard nailed to the wall, she found a large kettle. "Take this and bring back as much water as you can carry."

Sylvie and Fay appeared at the door, staring within. "I

found an old sheet and some towels," Sylvie said. "And a whole pile of soap. It's real perfumey, too. Maybe we could all take baths!"

"Can we go and explore the lodge, Auntie Zeb?" Fay asked.

"Later," Zebrina said. "Right now I'll need some nurse's aides."

"I'm going to be a nurse someday," Fay said.

"Very good, treasure. Now, let's see—Sylvie, tell the boys not to run off."

Sylvie rolled her eyes. "No danger. Lester's half-asleep on the floor and Patrick's in the big chair, snoring."

"Poor brave lads," Zeb said, laying kindling in the stove. Her eyelids sagged. Her ankles ached. She almost nodded into sleep standing where she was, and ruefully pictured Patrick ensconced in the fat, soft-looking chair. *Her* chair, a goal glimmering at the distant end of her tunnel of weariness. Selfish old thing, she accused herself, rubbed her cheeks with vigorous palms, and continued her round of duties.

A full two hours later, Zebrina sank into the now-empty chair, gave a final glance at the sleeping hunter and the new bandage showing on his leg in the twilight, and closed her eyes. "One half hour," she had instructed Patrick. "Then we'll prepare for the night." They were hungry, she knew, and she had little to offer them—except smoked venison. They would all have to put sentiment aside and avail themselves of the meat. Refusing would do nothing for the dead deer.

Now she breathed deeply, tranquilly, chin against her

chest, her own bandage begrimed with travel stains and
dried blood.

It seemed only a moment before Patrick roused her,
standing before the chair, consulting his watch. "Time,
Aunt Zeb."

She shook herself awake. "It can't be—I just now
nodded off."

"You said a half hour, and that's what it is. Boy, that
lodge is super! We went all over it. There's a big room
with a billiard table, and even a bowling alley, and at
least three bedrooms with beds with tasseled spreads. We
even found a big can of baked beans in the kitchen. I
got it open and we all ate. And we saw two cats—wild
ones. Fay says she's going to tame one, but they'll never
come near her."

"Probably not." She rubbed sleep from her eyes.
"Where's Knobs?"

"I'm right here, Auntie," Knobs said at her elbow.

"It is kind of spooky though, as Josh said," Patrick
continued. "Dust on everything, and it echoes when you
walk or talk. A great place for ghosts to hang out."

"Are there really ghosts?" Knobs asked Patrick.

Zeb struggled up from her chair. "Of course not. That's
pure imagination. Patrick's only being silly. Now, bring
the remains of the water in the kettle to the bathroom so
I can attend to my own bruised and battered person."

Mechanically she fumbled for the light switch on the
bathroom wall, and even felt an instant's astonishment
when no illumination came from the bulbs. Perhaps it was
just as well, she thought, straining to see her shadowy

features in the faint light from the bathroom window. Knobs returned and Zeb helped her empty the kettle into the wash basin. She soaked the dried bandage around her head and removed it gingerly. From what she could see of the gash, it was not deep. A ready-made bandage from the medicine kit would suffice.

She heard Josh groan from the other room. He was becoming feverish, there was no doubt about it, and his wound looked less promising than her first, harried glance had indicated. Further, there was no sign that the .22 bullet had exited, meaning that it might be imbedded in his anklebone.

He had brought it on himself, she thought, trying to harden her heart. Still, she had a responsibility. And poor Lester; the last thing on earth she would ever have wished on the boy. As it was, she feared that Lester's left wrist was fractured. She had noticed how he had used only his right arm in helping Patrick carry Josh. She must inspect it more closely and devise a splint, if need be. And she must see to their sleeping quarters, some food other than baked beans, if possible, and, above all, decide on their future course.

Sufficient unto the moment is the trouble thereof, she chided herself, and by an act of will gave herself to the extreme pleasure of lathering her face, neck, and arms with the "perfumey" soap Sylvie had found. Ah, how good water—tepid though it was—and soap were. And what a wonderful invention was the comb. Drawing it from a skirt pocket, she undid the snarls of her white hair, taking her time while Knobs and Patrick paced about restlessly at the front of the suite.

She felt refreshed as she joined them. Together they strode through the cooling night air toward the lodge. Lester was standing alone in the tennis court, his tall, lean figure diminished by the empty rectangle and the towering mountains beyond. His profile was toward them, his face inclined toward a cleared space that appeared to have once been a golf course.

Even when he heard their footsteps, he did not turn, but pointed and murmured. "There's an animal out there, but I can't make it out. It seems to be grazing. Like a deer, only it's whitish."

"An albino deer?" Patrick suggested. "I can't see it at all."

Zeb made an attempt to see the creature, cupping her eyes, but the evening shadows were too deep and too long. Knobs, also, peered into the distance and took a few timid steps forward before returning to grasp Zeb's hand again.

Lester turned. "It's vanished." He looked weary. "How's Josh?"

"Sleeping," Patrick said. "He doesn't seem to have any other guns around. I looked. And those bullet boxes on the shelf are filled with stuff like strings and buttons, and tobacco that he probably got from that wrecked cigarette machine we found in the lodge lobby."

"Even if he had a cache of bullets," Lester said, "it wouldn't do him any good with his rifle gone."

From somewhere within the lodge came the sound of Sylvie's and Fay's voices, then a scream. Fay burst out through the door under the CRYSTAL LODGE sign, hugging her arms protectively around her chest. "There's a bat in there!"

Zeb hurried forward. "Wonderful! Where's Sylvie?"

"She's got her butterfly net and she's trying to catch it. Ugh!"

"Well, she mustn't!" Zeb declared, limping forward on her still-aching feet. "Knobs, come along."

Knobs hung back, sharing Fay's fright although she had never seen a live bat. Zeb waited, then went on. Knobs had been brave enough, considering all that had happened. She could not be expected to become heroic overnight, though it was a disadvantage not to have her guiding hand.

Lester loped up the entry steps and held out his right arm. "Here, Aunt Zeb. It's pretty dim in there."

"A far cry from a blue butterfly," Zeb said, taking his elbow. "Darling, I must look at your wrist before bed. Surely Sylvie can't expect to substitute that little fluttering bat for a Lepidopteran. I understand her obsession, dear little girl. Her father couldn't care less, from what I know about him. Not even if she captured the extinct blue whale."

Lester said nothing, concentrating on guiding her through the door and into the empty, echoing lobby with its waterless fountains, empty sofas, and lightless, splendid chandeliers.

"Sylvie, dear?" Zeb called. Her voice bounced back from the paneled walls and heavy overhanging beams. "Sylvie?" she repeated more softly, knowing what Patrick meant by the word "spooky." A mammoth fireplace yawned at one end of the hall, charred logs still lying in the grate, as dead as the burned bones of an animal but giving off a fragrance of charcoal to blend with the acrid soot smell from the flue.

They turned where a hallway extended toward the right,

their steps muffled in deep carpeting that only here and there showed ragged spots where mice or other rodents had experimented with its fibers for food or nests. In a room off the hallway, to their right, was a creaking of floor boards.

"There," Lester whispered.

A last green ray of twilight entered through tall French doors in the room. Sylvie stood there, a silhouette against the greenish light, deaf and blind to their presence, the net suspended in her hand. There was a dark, pulsing blob within the net, and though Zeb could see only its lashing struggles, she knew what the creature was.

She stood silent beside a silent Lester. Sylvie's back was turned toward them. Pathetic child, pathetic hapless bat, she grieved, holding back, waiting.

Sylvie moved slowly toward the French doors, the green light making her seem like an underwater swimmer. With her left hand she experimented with the latch. One half of the double door opened, letting a current of air into the musty room.

The air smelled green and fresh, like a cut melon, Zeb thought, watching Sylvie lift the bottom of the cone-shaped net upward toward the wide hoop at the top. The action was vague to Zebrina's straining eyes, yet it stood out sharply in her imagination, the blurred outline of a shadowy hope. Yes! Sylvie was trying to free the fragile beast. But could she, now that the bat had helped to trap itself in the cunning net by its own thrashings, the membrane of its wings so easily torn? She saw Sylvie's hand dip down.

Bats can bite, darling, Zeb wanted to cry out.

There was a sudden winged, flapping shape against the dying green light, just enough of an image to let Zeb know that Sylvie had managed to free what she had so ardently caught. Zeb moved on down the muffled hall, pulling Lester with her. They rounded another corner and stopped.

"Bless her," Zeb whispered. "Never let her know that we saw."

"No," Lester said. His eyes shone in the gloom, gold flecked with darker gold, the shadow of his dark hair stopping at his blurred eyebrows. "It was a little brown myotis, I think."

"I wish I could have seen it better," Zeb said, then let her voice rise. "Well, now, to other vital matters— beds, food, and the morning. We should have brought the flash."

"There are dozens of candles," Lester said. He strode through what seemed almost complete darkness to Zeb, and returned with a silver candelabrum, its yellow spikes of wax unscorched.

Zeb reached into the pocket of her skirt, which was never without its precious container of matches. She handed the box to Lester.

The three burning candles illuminated the space and at the same time created grotesque shadows. Walking out of darkness, like a brown-and-orange moth attracted to a lamp, came Sylvie.

As if to belie the tearstains on her cheeks, she strove to make her voice light. "I wondered whose voices I heard just now. Where did Fay run to?"

"She joined us outside," Zeb said. "Something frightened her."

Sylvie looked away from them, her head down. "A bat," she said, her voice faltering in spite of her obvious desire to keep it steady. "I wanted so much to catch something." She swallowed. "And I did catch him. Only, then when I looked at him struggling—well, I let him go." She raised her remorseful eyes. "He wasn't hurt, Auntie Zeb."

"I'm proud of you, dear heart."

"Where's your net?" Lester asked.

Sylvie raised her chin in a familiar proud and determined gesture. "Back there. I don't want it any more." She brushed a lock of her long hair from her eyes and with a tone of dismissing the subject asked, "Where's everybody else?"

"On their way, I judge," Lester said, hearing Patrick's voice in the distance. "How's this for a mansion in the deserted wilderness? If people knew what it's like up here, maybe they'd have second thoughts about clinging to their Plexiglas skies."

"Don't even think about it," Zeb said. "There may be something in mental telepathy, you know."

"There is," Lester said firmly.

"I wouldn't have missed this place for the world," Sylvie said.

No, Zeb thought. Nor would she. Yet they must find their way back to that other world of monorails and humming current, astrodomes and false grass. For no one, not even the stubborn Josh, could live here long, or only at the expense of the wild creatures also struggling to survive. She thought of the deer haunch hanging above the ashes in the smokehouse, and recalled the taste of such meat as a child when deer had been too plentiful for their own good.

She had loved the meat then. Her mouth watered, even now. Well, she pardoned herself, she had not feasted on canned baked beans; she had eaten nothing since a hastily munched Nutro-bar.

The Squad was gathered around her now, waiting for decision and direction, their faces washed by the light of the candles.

"Somebody should stay with Josh," Zeb said.

Fay, golden-faced in the glow, said, "I'll do it."

"I was sure you would be the one," Zeb answered, trying to fit this Fay with the shy, nail-nibbling girl on the broken rocking horse in the attic. She glanced at the other flame-touched faces. All still young, but sliding over the edge into maturity and adulthood. She felt a vague pain in her chest. My children, she thought. But they would be hers for only a little while. Like Steve and the other earlier members of her Nature Squad, they would find their own paths, sometimes their own wilderness. But they were all brave and beautiful, after their own fashion.

"Maybe I should go with Fay," Sylvie said. "He might —it might be safer."

"I'm sure he'll do no harm," Zeb said. "But it's a good idea, dear. While you're at it, fill whatever receptacles there are with water. Tomorrow we'll refill the tank from the spring. Knobs, dear?"

"I ought to be the one to stay with him," Lester said, but so softly no one heard.

A hand groped for hers in the dimness, a very grubby hand. Knobs did not much like soap and water even when it was easily available. Zeb made a mental note to rectify this, once they were settled down for the night, and to arrange relief shifts for the vigil with Josh.

"Lead on," she said to Patrick and Lester. Stumbling through the shadows in the wake of the separate candle Patrick had brought with him, she permitted herself to dream about a master bedroom in the lodge, huge pillows, old but clean sheets on a wide bed, possibly even a cool wine cellar with a bottle of rich port lying sleepily on its side.

"Were there any canned beans left over?" she inquired of Patrick's back.

He turned, grinning. "Some. And two cans of sardines. I forgot to tell you about those."

"Very nutritious," Zeb said, thinking of the beautiful sardines glowing in rich oil. "To the kitchen department first, I think, Pat."

It was much later, all of the Squad except Zeb and Lester bedded down in the ample quarters, that she sat across from him in the large dining room, fitting a temporary splint to his wrist.

"I violated all my vows," he said, staring into the blaze of the several candles they had collected. "There's blood on my conscience."

"There is blood on everybody's conscience, dear. Hold still."

He gritted his teeth as she strapped adhesive tape around the slats of wood they had cut. "I think I'll go and sit with him the rest of the night."

"There's only one bed."

"I could use the big chair, or the bear rug."

"As you wish," she said. Fay and Sylvie had returned from their vigil and there had seemed no need to continue the watch over Josh. "Be sure you have covers, or a sleeping bag. As for me—" She stood up, all her bones and muscles sagging toward sleep. "Good night, dear."

A few minutes later and she was in bed, luxuriating under a blanket, a fat pillow under her head. Much though she loved a tent, or huddling in a sleeping bag under the stars, there was a great deal to be said for beds. She thought of Lester and his vigil. In the chair, or sprawled out on the murdered bear's thick pelt?

Tomorrow morning . . . She turned on her side, away from the window blazoned with moonlight, willing herself to think only of the little brown bat out of the net, its skinny arm-wings stroking toward freedom.

Knobs, in the twin bed nearby, murmured in her sleep, then sat up, eyes wide, but Zeb was past hearing or knowing. Naked except for the panties she slept in, Knobs crept to the open window. She was certain she had heard a whinny such as horses sometimes gave on television. Climbing up on a window seat, she looked out, searching the bright landscape. All was still. No horse, with wings or without, moved through the blue-and-silver quietness.

I heard him, though, Knobs assured herself. Maybe Pegasus didn't want to show himself yet and was only making sure that everything was safe. But he would appear, if the Squad stayed long enough. He would let her see him. Maybe only once, but that would be enough. She crept to the warm bed, gave each jack on the nightstand a ritual pat, and went to sleep.

# CHAPTER 15

ZEBRINA stood in the center of the broad, weed-filled lawn in front of the lodge, the .22 in her hands. She pointed the muzzle at the sky, fired a shot, counted off five seconds, then fired a second shot, and a third. It was a useless ritual, she feared, since she had repeated the signal often for four days in a row, and now there were only two bullets left in the rifle chamber. It was increasingly obvious that there was no one within miles to hear her, and apparently no sharp-eyed pilot anywhere in the sky to see the three smudge fires the Squad had built.

For the first time, a deep discouragement overwhelmed her. She had been foolhardy to ignore more modern kinds of equipment, relying on an old-fashioned compass and out-moded SOS signals. How she would welcome now the personal transceiver Steve had urged her to buy, so small it could be worn on one's wrist, yet capable of establishing contact immediately with emergency headquarters in any part of the world, and containing its own tiny position-and-direction-finding device. It had not been mere stubbornness or a clinging to earlier ways on her part. Transceivers were still expensive and she had weighed the cost of the instrument against the amount she contributed to Steve's college tuition.

Anyhow, it was foolish to weep over spilled milk. She was here with what she had. Only, the children were here too, dependent on her. Josh, also, his condition becoming critical. Did she dare send someone—Patrick?—out on his own to seek help? No, the risk was far too great. It was safer to cling here, even if they were reduced to grubbing wild-plant roots out of the ground for food. Steve knew her tentative timetable and, unless something drastic prevented it, he would find a way to reach them once he realized they were overdue.

She could not fight off her gloom entirely. Even her earlier faith in the signal fires had dwindled. The three fires stood in a straight line, hot coals covered with damp green conifer boughs and moist, rotten wood, giving off columns of white smoke that rose high in the air. Probably one of the chief virtues of the smudges, Zeb decided, was that it kept the children occupied in lugging fresh fuel to them, thus distracting them from their worry and their hunger.

Not that anybody was actually starving, she assured herself. Not yet. Or no one but Lester. He refused to touch the smoked venison, or even the dozen trout that Patrick had managed to catch with Josh's rod. The deer haunch was nearly gone. Although there remained a small supply of other dried meats—what kind she could not tell, never having tasted bear or raccoon, which she shudderingly thought they might be—it was not the kind of diet any of them was used to. It was far too early in the season for berries. As for greens, the weedy lawn provided some source with its abundant plantains, dandelions, and lambs-quarters. Cooked or raw, the greens were tasty, in her opinion, but the Squad made wry faces over their "salads," as she called them. Only Lester welcomed her concoctions.

Josh was a special problem, seeming to have no appetite at all. The lodge's pantry contained seemingly endless containers of coffee and tea. Otherwise, there were only a small tin of bouillon cubes and eight cans of evaporated milk. Zebrina carefully measured out the milk, diluting it with water, dividing it among the children and Josh. The bouillon she reserved for him alone, as his strength was failing rapidly and he only shook his feverish head when she tried to force thinly cut strips of venison on him. Most other edibles in the pantry had been devoured or fouled by rodents and insects. If things came to the worst, she had thought while looking sadly at a bin of flour spotted with mouse droppings, perhaps she could sift the flour free of such, but the thought was not entrancing. In the meantime, they would make do with the moldy hardtack she had found in one of Josh's cupboards.

Looking toward the stream that ran below the tennis court, she saw that Patrick was angling once more for trout. Lester was near him, searching for water cress.

Zeb walked toward Josh's motel unit, Knobs at her side.

"I sure hope Patrick catches some more fish, don't you, Auntie Zeb? Does it hurt the fish when the hook catches them?"

"I suppose, although fish are presumed to be low in the life scale and it's impossible to know what they feel, dear. Our pain-threshold machines don't tell us anything about it, that's certain."

"Sylvie says that they eat each other. The big ones open their mouths and *gulp*, they swallow the little ones."

"Yes," Zeb admitted sorrowfully and glanced at the apparently empty sky. Even if an air bus or helicopter were there, she would not be apt to see it, but she would surely hear it. There was no sound but the faint sigh of the wind in the tall pines, and the fainter rustle of the creek. From her vantage point she could see one of the many lakes that dotted the area, brisk blue in the morning light.

"I like it here," Knobs said, even as her empty stomach gave a rumble of hunger.

"I like it too, treasure." Under different circumstances, it would be a wonderful place for a vacation. Even as it was, the children had relaxed into laughter and gaiety as they filled the lodge with the clack of bowling balls, or played on the ragged golf course with golfing equipment they had found in a club-room locker. Only yesterday, they had discovered a still-usable rowboat on the shore of Crystal Lake, and Lester had cleverly carved out crude oars from two driftwood planks. And regularly they brought her reports of newly discovered animals—a tree frog, a ladybug, a porcupine. But to Fay's disappointment, the two feral cats had vanished.

In spite of her heavy concern over the Squad's predicament and Josh, Zeb felt her heart lift at the thought of the animals and the sight of the blue, unpolluted lake. Left alone long enough, nature would heal itself, even at the lower geographical levels where the worst devastation had taken place. But it was here in this wild, blue attic above the domed cities that animals and plants had their best chance for survival. Nothing could ever replace, of course, the thousands of coyotes, foxes, and eagles once poisoned by the government's predator-control units.

Before entering Josh's house, she lifted the cover on the water tank. Someone would have to replenish it soon.

"He's sleepin'," Knobs whispered as they entered.

"No." Josh opened his eyes. Their deep-green color reminded Zeb of the emerald-colored lake the Squad had passed on the way up. He looked less feverish than he had at dawn.

"How are you feeling, Josh?"

He shrugged his shoulders under a faded pajama shirt. " 'Bout the same, I guess. Where's Les at?"

"Down by the stream. Do you want anything?"

"Want to get up and walk and find some fresh meat. There ain't much meat left, you know—and no canned goods at the lodge, either."

"I know that, very well."

"Used to be canned peaches and tomatoes and soups—" He licked his lips. "After that, I had to depend on my gun. I was already getting low on meat before your outfit showed up."

"I'm sorry that we've had to raid your supplies," Zeb said. "But we'll compensate you, in time. Someone's bound to see our signal fires soon—and we'll get you to a doctor."

He looked at her. "You don't say."

"I do say."

"You're just wasting ammunition firing off that .22, grandma. You should be saving it for a raccoon or squirrels." He added defiantly, "Or a doe."

She ignored him. "Celeste, bring him some fresh water."

"If those kids had any gumption, they'd be out on the

hunt, or they'd go back and try to find my .38. There's still some bullets left for that. Lester's a good enough shot when it comes to hitting a man."

"He's sorry about that, Josh."

"Yeah. That's all he talks about nights when he's fussing around me." He looked toward the empty cot Lester had crowded into the space, and kneaded his dry forehead with thumb and forefinger. "He's a funny kind of kid. No need for him to sleep here every night like he does. I'll be fine, once I get my strength back."

"It would happen faster if you'd eat, dear." Inadvertently, the endearment slipped out. It was habit, and yet not altogether that. Her hunter, as she thought of him, was far sicker than he knew. "If you could force yourself to take some solid food—"

"Venison!" he said, and his eyes seemed to go out of focus. "Dead meat. So sick of it, grandma. And my teeth ain't good." He turned his face away. "You know something?" he mumbled to the pillow. "I ain't tasted an orange or a piece of bread in six months. Or ice cream. I always did love ice cream. Where'd you say old Les is?"

"Down by the stream," she repeated, thinking of how often he mentioned Lester. She knew, from observation, the way Lester devoted himself to the young man, leaping up to bring him fresh water, helping him onto the porcelain tray they had tried to make into a kind a bedpan, putting cool cloths to his head, and eventually taking over Zeb's chore of changing the bandages as needed.

"Funny kid," Josh said again. "Had a young brother like him, once. Got blown up when he stepped on a land mine

over in—" His eyelids drooped and his voice ended in a
rattling snore.

The pungent odor of the signal fires drifted toward Zeb.
"Let's fill the water tank," she said to Knobs.

Lester, carrying in his good hand a bag crammed full of
water cress, approached the spot where Patrick was casting
his line into the brook. He had almost reached the place
when Patrick gave a triumphant shout and pulled in the
line. A fat rainbow trout thrashed on the hook.

"Isn't he a beauty, Les?" Patrick said.

"Yes," Lester said tonelessly and turned away. Patrick
had to do it, he knew, but the sight of the gasping fish
sickened him. He was not a vegetarian—except for an ex-
perimental period when he had forsworn meat for three
months as a test of his own will—but eating creatures one
had seen alive and shining was another thing. It was the
same with the dried venison. Every time he was tempted by
his growing hunger, he kept seeing the antlered buck.

He munched at the overflowing bag of water cress as he
made his way back up the trailless patch of woods that
bordered the stream, studying the various kinds of vegetation on the way. In a few damp spots there were mush-
rooms, or possibly toadstools. He let them be. Zeb had
warned them, over and over, about the deadly poison of
certain fungi. He wondered about the kinds of roots Indians had dug up and eaten in times long past. Perhaps
Josh would know which they were, but Josh talked only by
fits and starts, or in such a rambling way that it was difficult to piece together the random bits of information . . .

bits about a dead brother, a horse he had lost, or about his being a school dropout.

Even the short hike toward the lodge made Lester feel weak. He sat down in a patch of sunlight, listening to the wind and the brook, recalling the single light plane that had passed over the distant ridges the day before. Or had it been the day before that? It was difficult to keep track of time. They had been at Crystal Lodge a week—no, five days. That, plus the three days on the way, amounted to a total of eight days in all. Aunt Zeb had planned on about a seven-day trek although she had carried food sufficient for a longer time. The Super-sentries had changed all that.

There were three available sleeping bags, Lester brooded. What if he took one and set out to try to reach the car? Although he did not have a driver's license, he could drive. Only, he needed the car keys. Aunt Zeb would never give them to him; he would have to steal them.

From attempted manslaughter to theft, he thought, and only then realized that the whole scheme was a desperate fantasy. Even a seasoned driver would be unable to negotiate the rutted road with only one hand. He looked resentfully at the splint and bandages on his left forearm. Perhaps he and Patrick together could reach the car and drive it near the military outpost to find help. Even though the Squad might be able to survive indefinitely, Josh couldn't without medical attention. But, if he and Pat failed . . .

His thoughts wheeled from possibility to impossibility and back again until he felt that his brain was a well-worn circular track. He stood up and started toward the lodge.

Only by reeling backward so sharply that he stumbled to one knee did he avoid treading on a ground nest hidden under a clump of brush. He remained kneeling, looking at the depression in the earth neatly lined with pine needles and grass, ten reddish-buff eggs glowing within. There was a flutter of wings nearby, a squawking cry. He raised his head and saw the plump mountain quail railing at him from a stump. The blackish, erect plume on the male bird's forehead nodded like a flower-tipped baton. On another roost was the bird's mate, her smaller plume waving frantically in time with her terrified cries.

Lester had seen stuffed specimens of quail, but never the living creature, and he felt awe and delight. How lovely they were, buttoned up in their neat coats of feathers, as if attired for some special formal occasion.

He looked again at the nest and the glossy eggs. Surely quail eggs would be as tasty as any other. He permitted himself to think of whipping them into a creamy froth for scrambled eggs, or simply cracked and fried, sunny side up. How nourishing they would be for Josh.

He leaned down, his right hand suspended over the eggs, fighting his horrible temptation. The birds cried at him again, their frantic notes hurting his ears.

A shadow fell across him. He started back guiltily to see Patrick standing beside him, a batch of trout hanging on a stringer made from a crotch of wood, one sharpened end strung through the crimson gills.

"What are those birds so excited about?" Patrick said.

Lester hesitated, then gestured toward the nest. "I was almost ready to—steal the eggs."

Patrick, his hands bloody from stringing the trout, stared at Lester in disbelief. "Come on, Les, you wouldn't ever do anything like that! What would Zeb say?"

Lester rose from his crouched position. "I said I was *almost* going to do it." He marched from the spot, Patrick following. "Let's not talk about it. Do you think we should try to make it on our own to the car? There are sleeping bags enough and one canteen, and we might, with luck, find some of our lost supplies on the way."

"Aunt Zeb said we should stick together."

"But what if it means—dying together here?"

They stood watching the columns of smoke from the smudge fires rise vertically, waved only lightly by the breeze.

"Somebody's bound to see those," Patrick said, "even though we are off the main flyway. The thing is, Les, I'm not sure we could find our way back down without either the compass or Zeb. Steve Thorson knows we're out here. He has maps."

"Yes, but he doesn't know precisely where we are. Aunt Zeb thinks the Lost Lakes target is at least twenty miles distant."

Patrick nodded glumly. "Anyhow, I'm glad I caught some fish. But I'd trade them for a beef roast any day."

The moon was nearly full, sending more light into Josh's hut than the squat, flickering candle provided. Even though the moonlight seemed motionless, it did move. He watched its progress, seeing how the silver shadows changed, some objects brightening, others receding into dimness as the moon followed its high arc. He wondered about the Colonizers up there, and about the Moon Mechanics apprentice school back in the Southwest Regional Institute. Most of the draftees hadn't minded it, nor even the thought of being sent off into space to help set up low-gravity monorails linking the first pressurized cities together.

He had hated even the words the instructors used to describe such things, even though they didn't expect him to be more than a mechanic's helper. Of course, they had talked a lot about educating him more, though as far as he could make out he wouldn't be doing much different work than an unskilled worker did back in the old days. Expendable moon fodder, some of the fellows had complained of their roles, but even they were keen about the crescent-moon insignia on the sleeves of their uniforms.

Not him, Josh thought, feeling a wave of pain sweep up his leg. If it hadn't been for the rifle and bullets his grand-dad had left him, he wouldn't have been able to make out up here. Granddad had left him a lot of other things, too— the know-how to live in the woods and off the land, and how to shoot straight. He had managed, even before the draft grabbed him, to spend summers all by himself in the Sangre de Cristos. Half his high-school years had been spent there, out of sight of the Truant Task Force.

He fumbled for the water glass on the stand, feeling giddy again. He knew as well as the old lady that he needed a doctor, but if they took him back where doctors were, then the Space brass would be after him again. There was only one good thing about it all—they would never send him to the moon if his leg was permanently crippled. Lester had maybe done him a favor.

The water did little to relieve the dryness in his throat, but when he held the glass against his forehead, it cooled his skin. Where was old Les anyhow? Josh searched the visible landscape, watching for the familiar, long-legged figure to come with his skimpy supper tray. Not that he was hungry, except for things that didn't exist here. He gave himself over to a dreamlike scene of himself sitting before a heaped-up dish of ice cream, his throat muscles aching.

It was then that he heard the sound coming in from the east and knew immediately that it was a VTOL. He propped himself up, craning around so that the three signal fires were clearly visible to him. Judging by their brilliant flames, the smudge material had been removed and replaced with dry wood. An intense, probing light swept the area, making even the moonlight seem a low-powered candle. He caught one flash of the rotor blades on the vertical take-off and landing vehicle and the winking identification lights on its cabin, and saw it settle down softly only a few yards from the middle fire.

He shrank back against the pillow, waiting for the first helmeted-and-booted figure of a military policeman to appear. He had been careful about building open fires, fearful of the searching eyes of the law. Now old Zeb and the kids had done him in for sure. They were worried about their own skins, not his. He knotted his fists weakly. Trapped. Well, he had always been. That was the way it was, and maybe it was as much his own fault as anybody else's.

At the sound and then the sight of the VTOL, Patrick gave a shout. "It's a Verty—right on the front lawn!" He raced out through the lodge door, followed by Sylvie.

Zebrina, behind them, peered at the craft. She had seen Vertys, so-called, on TV and Electravision, but she had not been near one before. The rounded body of the cabin, resting on leglike supports, looked huge, although the faint whir of its turning blades sounded scarcely louder than the drone of a bee.

"Patrick—Sylvie," she called. "Wait here. We can't be sure—of anything."

The two turned back, Patrick reluctantly. "I'll bet it's Steve."

"We'll hope so," Zeb said. "Stay close, Celeste, love." She reached for Knobs's hand.

They waited silently, watching. Finally a cabin door wheezed open, a step slid out and up from some invisible slot under the cabin floor, and a figure emerged. The powerful searchlights oscillating at the tips of the rotored wings, and a steady beam from the cabin's interior, flooded both lawn and lodge. The figure poised in the doorway was approximately Steve Thorson's height but was so enveloped in a bulky contamination suit, with a glass-and-plastic mask covering the lower part of the face, that identification was impossible. It was only when he stepped down and started toward them that Zeb relaxed. That was most definitely Steve's loose-jointed stride.

"It's Steve, all right," Patrick declared, "and somebody else." A second figure, also masked, had appeared in the cabin opening.

"How's everybody?" Steve's voice, or a fairly accurate facsimile of it, cut across the silence as he spoke through a metal honeycomb filter in the mask. "We had a heck of a time finding you—searched all around the Lost Lakes. What are you doing here?"

He and the Squad advanced toward each other until Zeb was close enough to make out his blue eyes and the freckled bridge of his nose.

"We had some problems," she said, "and blundered off course. Steve, dear, what are you doing with that silly mask on? Take it off!"

"You should be wearing one, too, judging by the electronic meters on the Verty. They're jiggling like mad, Aunt Zeb, registering all kinds of toxic residues—mutagenics, herbicides, nerve gas; you name it."

"Well, switch the foolish meters off, then," Zeb ordered, as if he were twelve years old again. "They've been brainwashed by that archaic government map. We've been here, Steve, for five days, and it's perfectly safe."

He regarded her thoughtfully, then shrugged and slipped the mask down against his chest. "I'll take your word for it, Zeb, but you'll have a lot harder time convincing Ed. Ed Collier of the Verty Service. He owns five Vertys and he swears by every instrument, button, and gadget in them —though, I'll admit, the meters on this particular machine are new and haven't been thoroughly tested." Steve smiled, came closer, and put an arm around Zeb. "As long as you're not contaminated, I'll let you kiss me."

"I was wondering how long I'd have to wait," she said, giving him a hug and an affectionate smack on the cheek.

"And, boy, are we glad you got here!" Patrick exclaimed. "We lost our food supply and we're about starving." He and the others gathered around the grinning Steve, firing questions at him while he tried to ask his own.

"You look pretty good, considering," he commented. "In spite of your enforced diet. Plenty of food in the Verty, and everything else. Ed goes loaded with supplies for every possible emergency: flood, fire, hurricane, or famine. Zeb, the doctor's going to compliment you on all those dropped pounds. And wow, look at Fay! We'll have to start calling her Skinny." He looked back toward the ship, calling out, "What's keeping you, Ed?"

Ed boomed back through his mask mike, "Just want to make sure everything's ready for take-off. How much time do the folks need to get ready?"

"What's he talking about?" Zeb demanded. "We can't possibly leave tonight. For one thing, we've a very sick man on our hands, and he needs attention right away. That's the first order of business, and then—well, there's the packing." The packing part sounded foolish in her own ears, but she simply was not prepared to move at such a pace as Ed Collier apparently expected. Of course, he undoubtedly charged for his services by the hour. Nevertheless, she was not going to be hurried. "Also," she added, "I'm not about to leave my perfectly good car stuck out there at the end of the highway, and I doubt that it will be too easy to find at night, in spite of your searchlights."

"Well—" Steve said, rubbing his chin. "Let's see. I'll talk to Ed about it. He's eager to get back for his first try at some deep-sea fishing. A bunch of marine biologists have discovered a clean ocean area up near the Aleutians. Not even any oil from the Trans-Alaska-Pipeline spill left there. And he has tons of fishing gear and other stuff he inherited from some uncle or other who used to be in the sporting-goods business. He figures there might be commercial possibilities— Well, look, I'll go get the med kit and check on your invalid. What's his problem, and what's he doing here?"

"Bullet wound," Zeb said. "Accidental."

Steve stared. "What's anybody doing with a gun up here? There's no game—is there? Or, even if there were, hardly anybody would bother to go after it these days."

Zebrina hesitated. The burly figure of the hired pilot was swinging down from the cabin. Masked to the eyes, as Steve had been, heavy shoulders and paunch evident even under his baggy suit, he seemed ominous. *Tons of fishing gear and other stuff. Sporting goods . . . commercial possibilities.* That included guns. Her spine itched, a warning signal.

"The weapon happened to be mine, Steve," she said. "I didn't mention it when I left home because I knew you would think I was foolish. As for the wounded young man —I don't know what he's doing here." Her myopic, squinting gaze held his. "Steve, darling, let's not talk about it in front of him." She nodded her head in the direction of the approaching figure. "I have my reasons."

"O.K., Aunt Zeb." Steve turned and met Ed Collier midway from the Verty.

Zeb struggled to make out what they said to each other. Frustration turned to relief as they both walked back toward the craft. When Steve reappeared, he carried what was presumably a kit of medical supplies. A few seconds later, the floodlights on the Verty flicked off and its hum ended abruptly, although there was still a glow from the cabin.

"Ed's bringing out the makings of a feast," Steve said as he paused beside her. "I talked him into staying. Which way to the patient?"

"I'll show you," Lester said. "Is it all just compressed food, or do you have anything fresh?"

"Two bona fide oranges, believe it or not, and a hunk of Swiss cheese. Why?"

Lester looked toward Josh's candlelighted shelter. "I think he'd like them."

A few minutes later, Lester strode swiftly ahead of Steve, the oranges and the package of cheese snuggled against his chest, envisioning Josh's pleasure. His own mouth watered at the thought of the food he carried, but he forced himself to think of other things—the flight tomorrow, the hope that Steve could turn the tide for Josh until he could be taken to a hospital, and Aunt Zeb's lie.

He recalled Ed Collier's inquisitive stare when he had requested the food for Josh. "How come none of you are wearing your masks?" he had asked.

"We didn't expect to need any, so we didn't bring them," Lester had answered.

"Could be a form of suicide."

"There's no danger here—" Lester had started to say and then thought better of it. "Maybe," he conceded, remembering how Aunt Zeb had cautioned Steve to silence.

"Here we are," he said now to Steve as they reached Josh's door, and the two went in.

# CHAPTER 16

ZEBRINA pulled off her boots as she sat on the edge of the bed, wriggling her weary toes. She had already extinguished the candle, after tucking Knobs into the bed opposite. Poor child. The others had found keepsakes—pine cones, rock samples, a porcupine quill. Aside from Knobs's having felt importance as Zeb's guide, and therefore some self-esteem, all Knobs would be returning home with was her boxes of jacks. Knobs had not mentioned Pegasus recently, but Zeb knew she had not relinquished her dream.

Zeb sighed and rubbed her eyes. Someone, St. Augustine, she drowsily recollected, had said that it was not important that certain mythical animals had never existed. What mattered, he said, was what they symbolized. Someday the mature Knobs would recognize the truth of that.

The pillow looked inviting, but Zeb sat as she was, mechanically massaging her ankles, remembering the night's "feast" in the lodge. It had been a feast, certainly, the dehydrated and frozen meats and vegetables responding to her efforts with the smokehouse stove so that, delivered to the table, they had seemed almost as glorious as fresh foods. Only then had Ed Collier relinquished his mask and she had been able to study the wide-jawed face behind it.

"Maybe my instruments are over-touchy, or need calibrating," he had conceded. "Nevertheless, Crystal Lodge is officially quarantined. Any fish in these streams and lakes around here?"

"I'll say there are!" Patrick had responded. "You should see the batch I caught today."

"That so?" Ed said and Zeb saw the gleam of interest in his deep-set hazel eyes.

She rushed into the momentary silence. "Yes—a shame that they were not edible. Mercury poisoning, it seems, mercury being all but indestructible."

"But—" Sylvie began, staring at her, while Fay blinked in astonishment.

"All very deceptive," Zeb hurried on. "The waters look pure and it's evident that the forests have managed to survive, but this is certainly no place one would stay any longer than necessary. The air does seem quite pollution-free—at least, we have suffered no ill effects—but it may be, Mr. Collier, that your subtle instruments are more than correct about the potential dangers. Won't you have some more of this beef? It's delicious."

He accepted a very small piece, and she noticed that when he left the table to go outside, he slipped his mask in place again.

The children had continued to regard her with wonder and perplexity but they had remained silent. Later, she had commanded them in her firmest voice not to volunteer any information but to let her answer whatever questions were asked.

Ah, what a liar I have become, Zeb thought now, fluffing her pillow. But she did not trust Ed Collier and his probing, inquisitive eyes, nor could she forget his inheritance of a once-flourishing sporting-goods firm.

"He's a go-getter," Steve had mentioned sometime during the evening when Ed was checking on the Verty. "He built his Verty company up from scratch, though with family money to start on. And he's farsighted, as with this notion that he might be able to recommercialize deep-sea fishing. He also thinks he might be able, with promotion and advertising, to seduce people out of their home complexes into—well, places like this. I doubt it. People have been too scared too long. Anyway, there are all the sports and entertainment anybody could ever need, right under the domes."

"You haven't told me yet about the babies," she had said, to change the subject, although she did want to know.

"Well and hearty, but lonesome. I cleaned Max Cat's ears, but he didn't appreciate it, and I treated your beloved setter for a touch of conjunctivitis. Otherwise, all's fine— I arranged for a colleague to care for them during my absence."

It would be good to see her pets again, Zeb thought as she took a final look at the moonlight. Patrick, Sylvie, and Fay had all expressed enthusiasm about the return home on the morrow. Only Lester had been more than usually silent, and she suspected that the cause was his realization that it might be a long while, if ever, before he could visit such wilderness again. At least, for him, there was a chance. For herself it was most unlikely. She had exhausted her strength on this expedition. And she had not been wise either at the beginning or the end, least of all at the end.

Her head touched the pillow, a vision of Ed Collier peering and poking around the grounds and the lodge obtruding itself on her attempt to relax into sleep.

We should have departed tonight, she thought, as Steve and the pilot had planned. As it was, the man had had too much time to survey the area. Perhaps he already suspected her of lying about the trout and the lack of wild game.

She clamped her eyes shut, praying that no deer and fawns, not even a chipmunk or a mouse, would appear before the Verty whooshed upward in the morning. A bird cried out in the silence. Ed and Steve, she trusted, were sound asleep in the empty motel unit they had elected to repose in for the night.

Knobs heard the bird's cry. But it was not that for which she had lain awake, pretending to be asleep. She remained still, restraining herself until she heard Aunt Zeb's deep breathing. Then she sat up, stiffly alert, listening for the whinny. It had come the first night, and the night after. Now for four nights there had been only silence except for the *crick-crick* of an insect, and the yelp, once, of some animal. She had crept to the window each night, searching the empty tennis court, the weedy lawn, the shores of the lake, seeking the snow-white form of the winged horse. Once she thought she had seen him but she knew, in her heart, that it had been imagination caused by a trembling of moonlit leaves, or the shine of a cluster of rocks.

If Pegasus didn't come tonight she would never have a chance to see him. And maybe the clumsy aircraft with its hum and all its winking lights had frightened him away forever. She wished she could stay here and never have to go back anywhere, except that then Aunt Zeb would go off with Steve and the others and it would be like hanging all by herself on the freeway fence again.

She had set her jacks on the table beside the bed, all except Silver Daddy. He stayed in the darkness of the box because he wasn't permitted to watch. But blue Bobby, red Rose, green Gary, yellow Yerda, black Barbara, and white William knew all about it. They stood in a row, waiting with her. Mommy, the purple jack, stood off to one side.

Knobs rose stealthily from the bed, shoulder blades and thin chest pale in the moonlight, and tiptoed toward the window seat. Crouching down, she sat watching, her chin in her hands, her breathing as shallow as she could make it.

There was silence except for Zeb's occasional sleep murmurings, the easy wind, and the ripple of the stream. She strained her ears for the faintest sound of a horse's neigh or the muffled sound of hoofbeats.

She stiffened. Something showed in the outside darkness, something glimmering white. At first she thought it was a patch of snow such as they had found in a crease of rocks. But then it moved. It came out of the darkness and stood gleaming against a black cloud of tangled vines and brush. It had four slender legs and a thick, silvery mane. It had wide nostrils and a neck that dipped downward. She could see its great teeth cropping the grass and weeds, and its tail, heavy as a broom of silk, swaying back and forth across its bright haunches.

It's him! she exulted silently. Pegasus! She could scarcely contain her breath, wanting to shout to waken Aunt Zeb and the Squad and the world. She held quiet, her arms crossed over her chest, hands clasping her elbows, shivering with the cool air and her own excitement.

Eyes fixed, she searched for a sign of his wings. The moonlight cast too many shadows for her to make them out clearly. They were probably folded tight against his sides since he didn't need them while he was feeding. Far off, Crystal Crag shone as if it were glazed with ice. Perhaps he had flown down from there!

She coughed against the chill air and pressed her hand against her mouth, but it was too late. Pegasus jerked his head up and for one heart-stopping instant she saw his moon-glittering eyes. Then, with a flick of his silken tail, a toss of his ocean-white mane, he lifted a hoof, pawed the ground once, and, with a leap so effortless it seemed the wind lifted him, he disappeared into the shadows.

Knobs sat motionless, staring after him, her heart knocking with wonder. He had finally come. He had seen her. He had stood in plain sight and he had turned his eyes toward her, looking at her as if he knew her. She would never, never tell anyone because no one would ever believe her. It would be her very own secret forever.

She crept back toward her bed. The pointed tips of the jacks gleamed dully in the light. She glanced at them with indifference. They were suddenly just ordinary jacks, all of them, even Silver Daddy locked up in his box.

Knobs lay back, looking dreamily toward the window. The stars were pale because of so much moonlight, but one star was far larger and brighter than the others. Maybe it was Pegasus's special star. If she could find the same star again, in Old City, she would ask Aunt Zeb its name.

She looked over at Zeb, the bulge of Zeb's body under the covers, the shaggy head half-concealed by her pillow. "I love you, Auntie Zeb," Knobs whispered.

She closed her eyes. It was all right to leave now. She wondered if the lemon tree had missed her.

Josh, too, had heard the whinnies several nights before, and he knew who had made them. It was Pete, the big stallion he had won in a dice game from a fellow in No-gales; Pete who had deserted him for a herd of wild horses. Having tasted freedom and the joy of a harem, the horse would never return except for a nibble of domestic grass and the bundles of hay still left in the lodge's stable. Josh had long ago given up trying to capture the wily beast.

Go on, be free, old boy, Josh thought. You're the luckiest one of all.

At dawn they stood ready beside the aircraft while Steve and Ed brought Josh on a stretcher from his cabin. He looked wan, Patrick thought, but not so feverish as before. After the doctors at New City removed the bullet from his leg, Aunt Zeb was going to keep Josh, she said, while he recuperated. And if he was a help around the house, and "behaved himself," maybe she would let him stay as long as he liked.

Would she let him sit in on the Squad meetings? Patrick

wondered with a twinge of jealousy, then dismissed the emotion as unworthy. He would remain the leader. If it weren't for him, Josh might still be lying there near the meadow. When Patrick flexed his back muscles he could still feel a touch of the soreness that had resulted from his climb that day, Josh a punishing weight over his shoulders. It was only when he could scarcely draw another breath, his knees buckling, that he had been forced to let Lester help him.

Funny, he mused, watching the men load Josh into the Verty, how before the trip he had often wondered what it would be like to rescue someone. He had thought it would be Fay or some other member of the Squad. And he had wondered if he could really measure up to such a task. Now he knew that he could, for he *had*. He deliberately flexed his back muscles to feel the twitch of pain. Pain and pride.

He watched admiringly as Steve swung down from the ship, ignoring the electric step that automatically lifted passengers into or out of the roomy cabin. Steve had picked him out to be co-driver on the rough road back, after Ed set them down at the spot where Aunt Zeb's old car stood. Of course, it was an inevitable choice because of Les's bum hand, and neither Sylvie nor Fay drove. Still, the way Steve had grinned at him and said, "If we get stuck, Pat here can put those hardy shoulders of his to the job and lift us out," had left Patrick with a warm glow.

"And, Patrick," Zeb had instructed, "remember to water that manzanita shoot on the way home."

Now she was nervously preparing herself, and everybody else, for the flight. "Darlings," she instructed, "you do exactly as Steve tells you. Sit where he says, and buckle yourselves in carefully, and keep calm."

Patrick grinned. Zeb was as fidgety as if she were about to take flight under her own power, pacing back and forth, fussing about their few remaining belongings, and in between times glancing suspiciously at the Verty. In spite of her scrubbed face and hands, her clothes were grubby—like his own, Patrick thought ruefully.

Ed Collier pressed a button on the instrument panel and the rotors at the tips of the angled wings began to hum. He stepped down and said, "Everybody ready?" He was no longer wearing his mask.

"Go ahead, dear," Aunt Zeb said, giving Sylvie a gentle push. "Now Fay." She looked around, face and eyes distraught, her helmet askew. "Fay? Oh, there you are, love. Hurry aboard now. Patrick. Lester?"

Lester stood to one side, apart, his eyes fixed broodingly on the sunrise making lavender domes and steeples of the surrounding mountains.

"Ready, Les," Steve called.

Lester moved slowly toward the craft, as if wading through hip-deep water. Steve and all the others, excepting Ed Collier, were now within the craft. Ed, like Lester, gave the landscape a final, speculative glance.

He spoke, his voice barely audible to Lester above the drone of the Verty. "That fellow up there on the stretcher has been feeding lies to you people—about the trout, and all the rest of it. He tried lying to me too, but I know he's managed to live up here for months, according to the evidence."

Lester felt a slight chill between his shoulder blades. "What do you mean?"

"There's a pile of trout bones out in the woods, and not very old, either. He's been eating them and telling you folks they were poisonous. Further, I found several deer skeletons, and two fresh hides, not to mention a bear's skull that's still pretty ripe." His gaze lingered on the lodge. "He's not the only liar. So are my instruments—though they can be adjusted—and the so-called environmental experts that have been scaring people to death. You know, it wouldn't take much money to make that lodge glitter. Then with some hot advertising on the media—Well, all aboard, chum."

Lester stood as if transfixed, the chill spreading throughout his body. "But you can't—I mean, you mustn't!" Ed Collier heard nothing, having already mounted the automatic lifter. He waved to Lester to follow, then stepped inside.

Lester sent a frantic glance back toward the wilderness, tempted to race away from the Verty, to lose himself among the mountains and forests and glean what he could from them before they were again despoiled, the wildlife threatened.

Aunt Zeb's anxious face peered out at him from the door. "We're all waiting, love."

Helpless, he stepped onto the lifter and felt himself borne upward.

The well-lighted cabin was circular, upholstered seats for the passengers arranged in a ring apart from the control section. Josh had a reclining seat to himself just outside the circle. The seat to Zeb's right was empty, Knobs on her left. Zeb beckoned to Lester, indicating the empty seat.

He walked woodenly toward it, almost unseeing.

"Here we are, dear," Aunt Zeb said as he stumbled toward the place and slumped down. She reached out and put her warm, broad-knuckled hand over his. "Don't forget your seat harness."

Here we are. Where exactly was "here"? A moment in time and space, vanishing even as he contemplated it. He looked out through the porthole window at the young forests that had thrust up to cover the scars of mining, resorts, and boom towns, and at the ancient trees that had endured even the worst assaults. He thought of the animals they had discovered—the Belding squirrel, the quail, the antlered buck. . . .

A chilling vision blurred the scene, a vision of billboards proclaiming: *CRYSTAL CRAG FOR THE ADVEN-TUROUS, America's Fabulous Frontier, Reclaimed and Acclaimed, Safe for Young and Old!* He imagined long lines of ground-effects machines gliding over the majestic slopes, crowded with tourists seeking a new thrill sensation; Verties with pontoons descending in hordes on the blue lakes; electric and turbine-driven cars streaming up a super-highway.

Fay nibbled a finger nail, watching Zeb. "It will be wonderful to get home. Won't it, Aunt Zeb?"

"But we'll come back again!" Sylvie declared.

"Yes—perhaps," Zeb murmured, trying to cope with both questions at once at the same time that she nervously watched Ed manipulating his various flight controls. She turned. "Are you comfortable, Josh, dear?"

He nodded absently, his gaze clinging to the landscape. Josh loves it, too, she realized, in his own way.

There was a gust of air, a vibration, and abruptly they were ascending at great speed. Zeb held her breath, waited, and then exclaimed with scorn, "Why, it's nothing much more spectacular than going up in an ordinary elevator, Squad." She leaned forward, straining to see out. "There's the crag—there's the lake—there's—" She sat back in sad resignation, for it had all disappeared in a moment.

Except for the whir of the rotors, the drone of the power plant, and some exchange of comments between Steve and Ed, the silence was heavy. She looked around her at the faces of her Squad members and saw the solemnity in each pair of eyes. Lester avoided her gaze, but she had already observed the troubled expression in his face. Even Patrick, seldom given to introspection, was looking before him in a brooding, almost melancholy way.

Knobs pushed her hand into Zeb's. "I know why you lied about the trout and things. So do Sylvie and Fay. We talked about it together. It was to keep other people from finding out about the animals and—"

"Sh-h-h, treasure," Zeb cautioned, looking toward the cockpit even as she thought how reassuring it was to hear solitary little Knobs use the term "we."

Ed Collier's solid shoulders showed against the cockpit glass, a vigorous silhouette almost blocking out a billowing, rose-tinted thunderhead beyond. He chuckled at something Steve said and Zeb thought: I may have misjudged him. He may have no plans in mind, or if he does, he might forget them even before we reach New City.

But there would be other Ed Colliers—as there had

been a Josh—each blundering into the reviving green worlds at various forsaken paradises on the earth.

Lester, she realized, was looking toward her now, his lips moving as if he wanted to speak.

"It will be all right, dear," she responded to the questioning anxiety in his look. "What is once experienced and loved, lasts forever." She cleared her throat against the undeniable ache there, thinking of future sessions in the attic, the shadows of The Heads, the sound of rain.

She had to break the silence, the funereal mood. Her voice cracking, she began the little song, "Good-by, good-by, be always kind and true—"

Sylvie joined in, then Patrick, Fay, and Knobs. Lester pressed his lips together, took a long breath, and then attempted to sing with them.

Knobs's voice had the most gusto. She remembered the great, winged horse in the moonlight. No matter what happened, she mused, Pegasus would always be there.

"Do you think the lemon tree got lonesome?" she asked Aunt Zeb at the end of the song.

"Perhaps, treasure," Zeb conceded. For herself, she concentrated on the memory of the doe and the twin fawns grazing at the edge of the gold-green meadow, the squirrel, the little bat, the solitary crow with his rough, black voice. Her sense of exhaustion and loss receded. She straightened in her seat, adjusted her helmet squarely atop her white hair, and stared ahead.

"We'll meet next Saturday, Squad, as usual," she announced, and ignored Ed Collier's shoulders, focusing with all the vision she had on the brilliance of the thunderhead hanging against the dazzling blue beyond.